EXILED FROM ALMOST EVERYWHERE

EXILED FROM ALMOST EVERYWHERE

(THE POSTHUMOUS LIFE
OF THE MONSTER OF LE SENTIER)

A NOVEL BY JUAN GOYTISOLO

TRANSLATED BY PETER BUSH

DALKEY ARCHIVE PRESS
CHAMPAIGN AND LONDON

Originally published in Spanish as *El exiliado de aquí y allá* by Círculo de Lectores,
S. A. (Sociedad Unipersonal)/Galaxia Gutenberg, 2008
Copyright © 2008 by Juan Goytisolo
Translation copyright © 2011 by Peter Bush
First edition, 2011
All rights reserved

Library of Congress Cataloging-in-Publication Data

Goytisolo, Juan.
[Exiliado de aquí y allá. English]
Exiled from almost everywhere : the posthumous life of the monster
of Le Sentier / by Juan Goytisolo ; translated by Peter Bush. -- 1st
ed.
  p. cm.
Originally published El exiliado de aquí y allá: Barcelona : Galaxia
Gutenberg : Círculo de Lectores, c2008.
ISBN 978-1-56478-635-7 (pbk. : alk. paper)
1. Satire. I. Bush, Peter R., 1946- II. Title.
PQ6613.O79E9513 2011
863'.64--dc22
                                    2010050133

Partially funded by the University of Illinois at Urbana-Champaign and by a grant
from the Illinois Arts Council, a state agency

This work has been published with a subsidy from the Directorate General of Books,
Archives and Libraries of the Spanish Ministry of Culture

www.dalkeyarchive.com

Cover: design and composition by Danielle Dutton, illustration by Nicholas Motte
Printed on permanent/durable acid-free paper and bound in the
United States of America

If only my style captures the whispers of the moment.

KARL KRAUS

EXILED FROM ALMOST EVERYWHERE

IN THE HEREAFTER

Just as he was leaving the wake for one of his acquaintances in the locality, the Italian barber on the corner (whose verbal diarrhea and constant recourse to clichés he preferred to dodge) smirked like a smart-ass and quipped: "The afterlife must be really wild, don't you reckon? As far as I know, nobody's ever tried to get back to this dump!"

The Forza Italia patriot got it totally wrong because, even when reduced to smithereens, he had decided he *did* want to return to the planet where a terrorist detonated the explosive device hidden in the lining of his gabardine, thus dispatching him and his book to the Hereafter. He suddenly found himself in a deserted cyber-café with thousands (millions) of computers and their respective workstations. A giant panel flashed on and off, tirelessly repeating the same message: VIRTUAL UNIVERSE. He didn't know what to do next or what was expected of him and roamed the void of infinite space until he flopped down exhausted in front of one of the keyboards only to see his own face on the screen, complete with hat and dark tinted glasses under the heading "The Monster of Le Sentier."

What else *could* he do but explore every opportunity offered by the data and information from the electronic galaxy and its vast array of programs to suit all tastes and ages? His memory when alive had been replaced by a new one he now played with, despite being so inept and clumsy, as the e-mails kept flowing in. He started exchanging messages (his caustic ramblings and fantasies) with visible or anonymous computer geeks who simply had to type in sentiermonster@hotmail to establish contact, attracted maybe by the puerile extremism and suspect nature of writing that you, my long-suffering reader, can now judge for yourself.

HIS FIRST STEPS

The knowing reader will wonder how a clumsy cuss like him, unable to open an umbrella or wind up a watch, was able to navigate his computer and communicate with both the world from which he'd been dispatched and the starry nebula of the Hereafter.

Death isn't what you think it is, dear friend: you'll find out sooner or later. You can just as easily find yourself in a cybercafé the size of an Olympic stadium as floating in the weightlessness of space, or helplessly trapped in a traffic jam with an objectionable Madrid taxi driver for company (whose monologue on human rights you'll get to hear later on in the book), or encapsulated in the meager gray matter of a scatterbrain who masquerades as a professor.

Fantasies I've cooked up? Come break the flimsy membrane separating us, and your very own virtual eyes will see the scatter-brain, the ineffable next-door neighbor of the deceased Monster of Le Sentier. Listen to her, my skeptical friend, as the pearls of wisdom pour from her small, straight-lined beak, and she shakes her flabby body and many-colored plumage.

"I'd already told you so a thousand times! They get everywhere like microbes from a plague! They steal and deal drugs to finance their terrorist attacks. I've just received an invitation to join a patriotic march and I'd like you to come. If we don't drop nuclear bombs on the countries they're from, all is lost: they will annihilate us!"

Don't try to plug your ears, soul brother. You have none. The latest whispers reach your mind without passing through the senses. The ether encompasses everything, even that trivial conversation.

LAUNDERING

Who'd give any credibility to the words of a dead man? The un-likely reader of these lines might like to see them off with a shrug of the shoulders and send them flying into the wastebin. But, believe me, it would be a mistake.

When we cross the fragile membrane separating us from the Hereafter, we are transformed, though we remain ourselves, as we gaze from afar at our tiny Earth and assess its puny worth. Seated in front of his computer, the Monster reviews messages and declarations from the place where time flew by that have mysteriously filtered through to his web page with its secret password:

Take a drive through the stinking masses in that limousine custom-made for you and the Chantilly Cream of the planet.

Contact the Wright-Patterson Air Force base in Dayton, Ohio. You'll love what they have to offer. An erogenous bomb custom-made for you!

As the list of suggestions is interminable, the deceased is moved in turn to write an e-mail to a correspondent he doesn't know, though he must be someone, he imagines, close to his own subversive ideas and unsettling sense of humor:

If love for the Holy Spirit can launder souls, why wouldn't the bank of that name launder money? If you are in agreement, contact us and send us your savings. The Paraclete guarantees a quick and handsome return.

Still fazed by the speed of cyberspace, to his surprise and astonishment, our mini-hero immediately receives a long epistle or, rather, a sermon. Unfortunately, the text is in Latin, and the only thing he can decipher is the e-mailer's signature: an enigmatic Monsignor.

NOSTALGIA FOR THE THEREAFTER

He inevitably went for a wander around his district. Nobody seemed to recognize him or stopped to say hello and chat about the weather. He tried to keep his distance from his old abode, wanting to avoid untimely encounters with his neighbors. He realized nonetheless that innumerable security cameras were filming him. Although his appearance didn't match the standard terrorist profile popularized by the media, his glasses and idiosyncratic gabardine, inappropriate for a sunny morning and the summer heat, might perhaps arouse the suspicions of the Intelligence Services. He sat down in a café near the Ludovicus Magnus Arch and lit up a joint. Before even taking his order, the waiter pointed to the sign prohibiting smoking inside and he threw his butt on the ground, embarrassed and shamefaced. His proverbial clumsiness betrayed him. He went down the nearest metro entrance, bought a ticket at the counter, pretended to consult the map, then decided against repeating his usual itinerary around promiscuous, potentially perilous alleys, and went back up to the boulevard's packed sidewalk. He was trying to shake putative stalkers off his trail and rehearsed the old route of the hero of *L'Éducation Sentimentale*, which had been transformed overnight into the general headquarters of the ultra-media-conscious President of the Republic. Given his marching orders by that man's muscular marshals, he turned heel and unexpectedly bumped into a May '68 philosopher, his wavy hair graying, topped by the halo of a court adviser.

Listen to him, dear reader.

WHAT GUY DEBORD HAD TO SAY

Quick! Off to the studios! I've had an idea! I must tell it to the cameras, grab the media's attention with a massive press conference! How can I develop the thread of my thoughts if nobody is listening, if nobody is looking at me? The batteries to my brain run out and it stops working! Who can speak in a void and display the renowned sinews of his intellect if he doesn't enjoy that stimulating contact with the public? The image of my very own self projected live makes the energy and brilliance of my speech fizz and sparkle. Ever attentive to my consultant's advice, I rest my chin on the palm of one hand and sink into a brief yet luminous meditation. My virtual audience holds its breath. I hesitate, debate, convince. I am a luscious mix of Socrates, Nietzsche, and Pat Robertson.

NOW YOU JUST CAN'T REFUSE THE BEST BARGAINS

The Internet weirdos popping up on his screen were driving him crazy, as no doubt you are too, indignant reader, with all your put-downs of his manias and obsessions, the selfish limitations of his world, his fondness for beating shoe leather around the backyards of his barrio, his dearth of interest in the vast universe out there, in short, his oppressive routines and blinkered vision. Why always the same walks, the same backstreets and squares, the same gray landscapes reiterated *ad nauseam*? Had he never heard of the exhilarating alternatives within the reach of whoever fancied them and had the means? Just contact one of the travel agencies promoted on the web; consult the offers plastered all over their stunning visuals! What about a cruise in the Baltic with stop-offs in Stockholm, St. Petersburg, and Riga? Or a trip around the Med and possible guided visits to the Coliseum, the Parthenon, or the mind-bending ruins of Carthage? Or, if he didn't fancy any of that, given his pathetic lack of interest in the Hanseatic League or the glorious ruins of Greece and Rome, how about a safari in Kenya or an exciting jungle trip along the Amazon? Or might he not find Bali, Machu Picchu and the Yucatán at all tempting? Or a foray into Patagonia and the remote Antarctic? The bargains kept coming onto his screen and the fantastic prices danced round his poor head, giving him a headache. A five-star hotel with gardens, swimming pools, and paddle courts! A double cabin, children free, with views of the coasts of Cyprus, Tunisia, and Egypt! A thousand-and-one-nights hotel in Taroudant or Ouarzazate! But it all simply ricocheted around his atrophied brain, certain as he was of the futility of changing locations. He thought of Nerval, Flaubert, and their fellow partygoer Maxime du Camp. Travel broadens the mind, opens you up to the Other, to the dialogue between cultures! He finally opted to choose blindfolded. Chance, he conjectured, would put him on the right road.

THE EROS BOMB

Military scientists working at the Wright-Patterson Air Force base in Dayton, Ohio, requested funds from the Pentagon to develop chemical agents that would arouse irresistible lust among the enemy infantry once they were spread across hostile airspace. The so-called erogenous bomb contained aphrodisiac substances to trigger off collective homoerotic behavior and seriously undermine the defensive capacities of the country targeted.

Our hapless hero was alerted by an e-mail and started to daydream. His life was uniformly gray, his horizons zero. His exchange of porno messages with the long-suffering angels of Sodom didn't stir him from his lethargy and he trawled the lethal ennui of cyberspace despairing like Munch's *Scream*. Only lurid scenes of a collective orgy of the soldiery could bring a glimmer of light into his deadly routine. One fine day, he decided to offer his services as a guinea pig in that heartening experiment. It wasn't at all easy to identify the necessary target. The many debates on the Axis of Evil never resolved which component would be the first plausible objective for a preventive strike. He took it upon himself to scout the territory and traveled to the riskiest states. The martial airs of the guards of the central command in one such nation quite bewitched him. He took his vitae to the Intelligence Services office, introduced himself as a qualified interpreter and was sent to a sensitive, high-risk zone. Providence, ever magnanimous, landed him in a barracks full of idlers twirling their mustaches and scratching their groins. He imagined the moment when, under the bomb's impact, they'd drop their weapons and flourish their scepters at him. He tried to slip between the best endowed, anticipating a blessed epiphany. In the meantime he tolerated the fiery heat of the desert wind. The days passed slowly and monotonously, punctuated by changes of the guard, reveille, and grub up. None of those brawny youths paid him the least attention. But, fully absorbed in his erotic fantasy, he didn't despair. He gazed at the horizon and waited for the rockets that would spark off the massive saturnalia. In the black of night he stuck on his night vision goggles and imagined every star bore the tail of the desired artifact. He begged the almighty heavens to let it be soon. Nevertheless, his glorious paradise faded like a mirage. As months, then years passed, he adopted a turtle's sluggish torpor. His dreams dried up on him. Though he *did* manage to come out of hibernation and return to his neighborhood where he initiated a lawsuit against the Armed Forces' laboratory for fraud and breach of promise. He received support from various humanitarian associations and Third World collectives, but awoke from his dream the night before a people's jury would declare in his favor.

A NON-ECO-FRIENDLY CADAVER

On his cyber-screen he followed the rebellion in the suburbs (cars set on fire, trash bins turned over, angry graffiti, angry half-breeds), prelude to the dynamic intervention of the forces of order with clubs, hoses, tear gas, and rubber bullets. Given the record of the individual concerning us here, the candid reader will predict that he was highly delighted. Not so. On the contrary, he experienced a vague sense of fear: fear he might be accused of the intellectual authorship of these acts. Hadn't he imagined all this in the pages of his tatty manuscript? The contacts he'd had with extremists of every stripe could be trawled by any cybercafé lurker, exposed on the Bishops' radio wavelength and the heavenly seraphim alerted. He was consoled by the thought that his book had remained a reluctantly private affair. He recalled the distant exchange with his publisher and his perfectly reasoned arguments. Such complete lunacy could only interest half a dozen idiots like him, who shared a sickly fascination for his grotesque fantasies. Why didn't he write stories that hooked the reading public and thrust him to the top of the best-seller lists? An action-packed cliffhanger with mafiosi, esoteric sects, secret rituals, and apocalyptic prophecies! The whole caboodle seasoned with age-old vendettas and sex, lots of sex! Rather than being a Mr. Nobody, he could be a rip-roaring Mr. Somebody, autograph thousands upon thousands of copies, and attain the fame and fortune of those who know how to win the hearts of their readers.

· Wise words, but on the late side. The Monster is dead and a non-eco-friendly cadaver is pushing up the daisies in some remote, shadowy cemetery that cannot possibly be pinpointed. As for his double in the Hereafter, the reader knows what to expect. Life has taught him nothing: he still can't tell the wheat from the chaff and earns a much-merited prize of hostile silence.

SPAM

At eleven months he loved to practice his scales. By the age
of three he discovered a precocious liking for classical ballet
and figure skating. By four, he was rehearsing his choreography
of *Swan Lake* and gracefully performing the lead role. Soon af-
terward he won over the viewers in a TV competition with fan-
dangos and *soleares* that became a worldwide hit bringing him
international recognition. In the meantime he'd memorized
The Little Prince and created his own dance troupe. Shortly after his seventh birthday, a man in and out of police cells, you
stood by the exit to the School for the Dramatic Arts and displayed your very own piece to its innocent pupils.

"Look how long mine is! Anyone fancy a feel?"

The little cherub volunteered straight off.

Remember that, my dear?

(Signed: Monsignor)

Become a pirate on the web, forget about patches over eyes or wearing a black armband in mourning. We will provide you with access codes to the centers of cyber power so you can infect them with a lethal virus that's impossible to detect. Keep the instructions from high command in front of your computer. Our skull and crossbones aren't from any adventure film but are the symbol of the final destruction of the System. Your contribution could be vital.

(Signed: The Virtuously Violent)

Are you one of them? Course you are! You like the Tool between your buttocks! You dreamed of playing the piano and ended up tinkering with something much sturdier and firmer. Our services filmed you with three undercover agents and recorded every one of your lying insinuations against our beloved Benefactor.

(Anonymous)

QUESTIONS, QUESTIONS, AND YET MORE QUESTIONS

Requests for explanation or clarification from the Hereafter piled up, jamming his mailbox. Was it a real or unreal, abstract or material, subtle or raw world?

But the philosophical preoccupations of some interlocutors disappeared into a morass of ramblings spawned by a literal reading of the Scriptures: had he seen the apple tree into whose tasty fruit Adam sunk his teeth when prompted by his spare rib? fucked gratis virgins with snowy white breasts and tumbling black tresses? interviewed the angels rescued by the Lord from their risky mission in the Axis of Evil or, rather, the Evil Eye, so lusted after by lewd sodomites?

Other messages simply set out the fantasies of his correspondents in the Thereafter (theirs, not his), copied from Las Vegas,

Benidorm's Terra Mítica, or Disneyland: theme parks with Egyptian pyramids, Buddhist temples, Roman statues, aquariums, zoos, waterslides and even a little, canvas-topped train driven by a woolly hatted Mickey Mouse!

The deceased inhabitant of Le Sentier doesn't have the strength to deal with such stupidity. Humanity disgusts him. We will take advantage of our ability to penetrate into his bewildered mind to reveal our first findings to the reader: his dream of being recruited by a radical organization and perpetrating lethal bombings.

TOTAL HARASSMENT

Like an elephant on a road island besieged by the sound and fury of the traffic, his existence on Earth had unraveled in an atmosphere of fear and threats. Everything around him was suddenly fraught with suspicion. His neighbors spied on him, his telephone was tapped, and his letters had clearly passed through the censor's hands. Although he moved from the district, persecution proliferated. He felt it in the distrustful looks from straphangers in the metro and the knowing winks exchanged by passengers jostling him in buses. When he went into a busy café, conversations came to a halt. Gazes converged on his person with evident disapproval. One bad day (and there was no shortage of bad days), the waiter brusquely asked after his sexual preferences or bantered with other customers about whether he'd come with high hopes of picking up the mustachioed Turkish cook or had a date with one of those young fillies who appeared in his wretched book. Indeed, hadn't Big Brother's Eye caught him on his micro-cameras jerking off in the public bathrooms in the Thereafter, or when he defecated (because one even defecates in the Hereafter, ingenuous reader), and blackmailed him, threatening to unload those filthy images onto the net? He didn't have a clue as to who was behind this hateful conspiracy. People did everything he asked without demurring. Everyone was in the employ of the System!

Like that hapless delinquent from a city slum wielding a rusty sword, ready to emulate the feats of the Prophet or that regiment of Polish cavalry launching into a gallop against the tanks of the Wehrmacht, his attempts at self-defense had been a fiasco. He used the Internet to contact radical cells of a different stripe that were nonetheless united in their hatred of Power: Basque Sabino's heirs, Shining Pathers, Grapos, Al-Andalus Jihadists, and other groups with murky acronyms but clear objectives. An e-mail signed by a mysterious "Alice" raised his hopes:

> I will spare you so many unjust wrongs, and, if you follow my instructions to the letter, you shall find peace.

CONJECTURES

Who was "Alice"?

Reader darling, we don't have the slightest idea. Our insights are ambivalent even though we now enjoy the advantage of being on the other side of the barrier. The first leads pointed to a well-known TV preacher, renowned for his mellifluous visions inspired by the saying "Suffer the little children to come unto me." Then they suggested a sect of devil worshippers and, finally, a would-be radical imam fond of offering advice of the "sin and sin hard, martyrdom will redeem you" kind.

Our poor scribbler contacted him via his computer. He expected to see a bearded guy wearing a biretta on his screen, proudly flaunting every single hair covering his chin and cheek, but found a flabby female in her forties, luridly face-packed and mistress of a *recherché* English she'd learned in her Oxford college.

"Elementary, my dear Monster! Looking like I do, nobody suspects me, and they assume I'm Al Kaaba rather than Al Qaeda!"

She laughed at her own wit and forwarded her plan of action, translated into twenty languages from Basque to Urdu.

"These are instructions for manufacturing explosives, dirty bombs, sarin gas or polonium 2010. You can follow them easily in your own home, taking care, naturally, not to attract the attention of your neighbors. Dress like me and nobody will notice you. The police are ubiquitous and can trace your whereabouts. Don't trust your cell phone: they always give you away. Constantly change your alias and web page."

The figure of "Alice" faded from the screen and the exiled from the Hereafter began to memorize the necessary means to secure his objective, but soon got into a muddle, as he did on that distant day when he read the instructions for winding his new watch, giving up his attempts after it shattered on the ground, finally taking a sedative.

Time and again redemption through martyrdom eluded his grasp!

HARD TIMES

Why couldn't the astonishing innovations at work in the field of genetics be applied to the novel? The genes determining the static identities and solid characters that peopled the world of your childhood no longer parallel the discoveries made by science. Hapless humans are the children of chance and circumstance, change accordingly, evolve or backtrack and switch personalities. A devout man, a classic "holier than thou" guy, may be at once a consummate pedophile (no shortage of candidates!) or the lethal agent of some crusade or jihad. The Monster of Le Sentier is a good example of that. Turncoat and lunatic, subject to capricious whims, he has transformed into someone different ever since he tired of his status as a parasite. He delivers inflammatory sermons in the local mosque, visits nearby parks hiding his stiff scepter under his gabardine, prowls in search of hirsute, weather-beaten immigrants in unholy places, and parodies the patriotic speeches of his barber—a paladin of Forza Italia!—or some bloodthirsty tyrant continually reelected unanimously by the People.

His sudden shift to the Hereafter has made him more suspicious, though it hasn't entirely swept away his inclination to extreme radicalism. Quick and deft like a conjurer, he changes disguise and shifts to the personality that suits his perverse fantasies. He could easily put himself into the shoes of an upstanding, altruistic citizen and win his reader's goodwill: a typical Jewish or Armenian wholesaler, an assimilated Muslim, or the member of some solidarity committee against poverty and discrimination. But nothing of that ilk fits his acerbic vision of the universe and the blinkered horizons, not to say blindness, of the individuals that populate it. When he wakes up, he looks at himself in the mirror and prepares his disguise for the day—these rites and customs survive into the Empyrean mists where he's been relocated! Beard and biretta; rouge, eyeliner, and wig for his "Alice"; gabardine and tinted specs for the exemplary suspect. Then he reviews the news on the Internet, looks for items to spark his imaginative gifts, and establishes the day's plan of action. An interview with the philosopher who votes for the right out of loyalty to the left! The massive "yes" vote in the referendum! Slick ads for an item aimed at the beautiful people. A fantastic Golf Open.

The political parties' election promises and offers of nonstop progress bring bitter laughter to his lips. The powers that be allied on behalf of the bricks and mortar that will destroy his childhood paradise provoke sarcastic humor rather than melancholy: and the first shalt be first in the kingdom of cement!

The Monster rubs his hands and prepares the relevant speech or comment that you, faithful reader, will find in the following pages of this book, that is, if you don't drop it and break a toe in the process.

You're canny and astute and, as you will have guessed by now, the deceased is a nihilist ready for a piece of the action.

CONTROLLED BY THE SYSTEM

From within the virtual space of that limbo cruelly deprogrammed by His Holiness Benedict the Antiquated, the Monster shrinks as he witnesses the collapse of the utopias from his era, sidelined by the would-be pragmatism of sustainable development, but belied daily by the worrying accumulation of thick cirrus or stratus clouds on the tiny planet where he lived to no profit.

He roamed his neighborhood like a sleepwalker, stopping in front of his barber's to inspect the image of the Forza Italia hero, carefully framed by his fan the barber, or the portrait of some dictator sitting on a huge gilded throne, unanimously and quinquennially voted in by his subjects. His questions remained unanswered and he walked warily searching for traces of "Alice." The fundamentalist imam left via the back door of the temple where he preached and, thanks to his vast repertory of disguises, went to clandestine meetings with the so-called Martyrs of Al-Andalus or the Anti-System Commandos of a mysterious Trotskyite splinter group. It was never revealed if "Alice" was his presumed spiritual guide or merely a self-projection. Who followed and who was being followed? Were the infinite security cameras installed in the district taping him or the other guy? Big Brother's single eye erased the differences between the two and stuck them in the same group of suspects. He (who?) took advantage of the confusion created by the impatient hoots from the traffic jam to revisit a passageway redolent of faded Baudelairean splendor and, after grinning idiotically at a group of Chinese traders, he bumped into him, or rather, himself, easily recognizable in hat, gabardine, and tinted glasses. A growing number of onlookers stared at him and he could hear their cackling chorus: there he is, there he is!

Fortunately his barber-friend's spiel got him out of that one.

DEMOCRATIC REFLECTIONS

I am a past master at the art of inflating budgets, handing out posts, and manipulating figures. I lie on camera with consummate ease. The public knows all this and admires me. That's why I was elected president and will be once again because ordinary citizens identify with my character, my fondness for power and money, and the bold pirouettes of my campaign. He's what we'd like to be, they tell themselves. He's inviting us to imitate him. If he now owns factories, companies, television channels, newspapers, and football clubs and rakes it in from all sides, we'll adopt him as our model. This is the essence of yours truly on the election trail: recognize yourself, look at yourself in the mirror! In five years your holdings can also increase tenfold, if not fifty-fold! Gone are the days when people talked about honesty, transparency, improved social services, and other cant from the stupid, empty-headed Left. The man in the street knows what's good for him, elects the clever guy, and cuts to the chase. My barefaced audacity and various antics boost the popularity and practical appeal of my pledges. A vote for me is a vote for you. I'll take up the challenge yet again! I'll be everybody's president because we all belong to the same body! I will continue in the breach for another five years, at the forefront, long live our freedom and the nation.

PUT YOURSELF IN THEIR SHOES

If someone could think for a few seconds before perishing as the victim of a terrorist attack, he would probably direct these last words at his executioner: Who are you, why blast me? He would put himself in their shoes, try to understand the reason or non-reason behind their action, and there's no better way to do that, so the experts tell us, than to follow step by step the chain of events and circumstances that led the perpetrator to espouse extremist ideology: that murky route that goes from the apparently normal lad (a youth like any other, sociable, studious, loved to play sports) to the individual ready to blast to bits any person designated by his chiefs or, if it's deemed necessary, a hundred un-recyclable souls, by simply detonating his device.

Our deceased in the Hereafter enjoys this extraordinary privilege: he can investigate the motives of those who made scrap metal out of him, and strive to follow the logic of their mental processes. Since every action is driven by a cause, he tells himself, recalling his distant schoolboy years, he must identify the latter and put aside humanitarian, politically correct considerations.

Absolutely convinced the violence stems from ideological premises and emotions fanned by identity (religion, nationalism, ethnicity, hatred of the oppressive state and its puppets), our beater of shoe-leather seeks info on the net. He believes his support for the struggle against the System must be total and unconditional. He flicks through a set of biographies of Utopians, philosophers, and saviors of the fatherland. He listens to a fiery "Hosanna, oh Osama!" and a CD by the Texas Rancher Trio. The binnacle magazines of Jihadists, Grapos, and Etarras fascinate him with their radical therapies. He sits in front of his computer and tries to download their programs and awaits the agreed-upon sign from "Alice" to initiate himself in the more practical tasks of the subsequent stage.

A JUDICIAL FARCE!

When I arrived at the apartment belonging to the art dealer whose legitimate execution made me a victim of this sinister judicial farce, I immediately told him I belonged to the Commandos for the Liberation of the Classes Oppressed by the System and set out the aim of the mission I'd been assigned: the expropriation of a precise quantity of money, in ratio to the global figure of his holdings, under the rubric of a revolutionary tax. I told it to him straight the second I pointed my weapon at him. I told him our fighters are under orders to execute those who, selfishly, devoid of social conscience, refuse to pay; rather than responding reasonably to our demands as laid out in the manifesto my left hand was offering him, demands that are crystal clear and impossible to refute, he attempted an aggressive feint and I was forced to give him a mortal blast. It was no mugging or crime, as the lackeys of the System claim, but the execution of a righteous sentence based on the principles of our cause. Death or victory! Valiant Commandos at the service of the People, we shall never surrender!

GOTCHA!

First he stood in front of him, looked round at his colleagues, and then wagged an accusing index finger.

"Look! Here he is! It's him for sure!"

Was he about to say, like a compatriot of his in the Thereafter, "the author of *Blood Wedding*"?

"The Monster of Le Sentier!"

"Madame . . ."

"Forget the froth and get to the point! Are you, or are you not, that loathsome character, accomplice to terrorists, who opens his gabardine and flashes his marks of identity at minors of either sex?"

"Come, come—what . . ."

"Aren't you ashamed to behave in such a way and then have the nerve to boast about it? A Swedish professor has sent me an e-mail with a list of pathetic acts that you yourself have described and endorsed. And, to top that, your scribblings defend the Islamist fifth column now invading us! Don't you see that we are facing a historic challenge, the outcome of which will determine whether our values have a future or not?"

He addressed his colleagues again, seeking their approval.

"Here you have him! Complete with gabardine and tinted glasses! Have you got a date with some bearded guy, or are you off to the park to pervert innocent children with the bait of your little white mouse?"

"I can assure you . . ."

"Nothing could be clearer! Only a monster like you could relish such indecent acts! If it were up to me . . ."

He reached into his pocket to show this man the death certificate signed by the judge the day he was bombed to bits in a small square in the area; they added his subsequent awkward, impulsive lunge in self-defense to the already lengthy list of charges.

"Watch out! How dare you try one of your lewd tricks on me and attempt to show me your pride and joy? I shall go to the police station immediately. Understand?"

Mercifully, a glitch in the electric circuit blacked out the computer screen.

A WARNING TO THOSE WHO JUMP TO CONCLUSIONS

If the kings and priests of yesteryear flaunted divine attributes in order to strengthen their grip on a timorous flock, today's state-of-the-art gadgets for spying on people and keeping them in line allow power to be exercised with means that are infinitely more efficient than the sacred, though fallible, invocation of the Lord. The cutting-edge technology at our fingertips enables us to detect, with absolute success, the slightest hints of discontent shown by individuals averse to the democratic advances forged by our President, the Father of Our Nation. Microscopic cameras, ubiquitous bugging devices scrutinize and record everything that happens in the domestic space of every member of the citizenry, from the matrimonial bed to the john where they satisfy their most intimate needs. Whoever dares to challenge the Boss and stand as candidate in an electoral contest that they have lost before it has begun must face the fallout from such rash lunacy. Endless images taken while he settles his buttocks on the toilet bowl, tenses his jaws and stomach muscles, sticks his index finger up his anus to facilitate the exit of fecal matter, and then checks the weight and size of the final emission, will be uploaded to the web and put out as breaking news on peak-time bulletins. Countless surfers and television viewers will watch in delight as he punctiliously rubs his nether eye, glances askance at the brown smeared paper, and stands up to evaluate his stools with an expert's learned eye. A voice-over will comment sarcastically: Do you really want to vote for a fellow like this? You will hear an answer come in the form of a sidesplitting guffaw. This wretch deserves outright rejection by the whole populace! Go with the People to his house and express your anger! Close-ups of the masses gathered on his doorstep, a frenzied sea of flags and photos of the President, and that voice-over again: Our President anointed will never be defeated! Everyone chorus it to the baton of the Father of Our Nation!

Much to the surprise of our man in exile, dear reader, the Internet message you have just read comes with his own e-mail address. What devious spirit can be pursuing him through the virtual galaxy of cyberspace?

ELECTIVE AFFINITIES

When searching the web for explosive experts ready to sacrifice their lives and sign up for the crusade, "Alice" received a mail from that Swedish professor. She wanted to contact her urgently and inform her of the list of charges against the Monster of Le Sentier, in order to fill in the background and help organize his defense. My country is a lawful state and one must abide by the rules. As a woman, you will grasp the gravity of the allegations. The personal knowledge you have of such tragic acts will corroborate my evidence most pertinently and must be put before a court of appeal.

Like a wily fanatical preacher, used to double-crosses and other counter-espionage ruses, "Alice" appears on screen in diva face-paint, dipping décolleté, and straw hat.

"Good morning."

"To you too."

"I'm not sure if you are aware of my studies of . . ."

"Yes, indeed I am."

"I would like to assemble first-hand witness accounts and I thought . . ."

"It's a huge list!"

"In my thesis on the subject I develop the theory about the pedophilia he simulates to mask his recourse to male prostitutes with that well-meaning stricken conscience displayed by those same middle-class Westerners he so likes to criticize and slander."

"I'll keep a close eye on his every step, darling. When I've completed my investigation, I'll let you know."

"I would also like to investigate the trips he goes on and his possible relationship with extremists."

"Don't be impatient, my cutie. I've been keeping tabs on him."

"Gender equality is an inalienable democratic right."

"Put your trust in me. I am a fundamentalist feminist. All the religions of the Book endorse the truth of what I say!"

(Our hero cowering in the ether signals a timid show of disagreement with a negative wave of the hand.)

MORE E-MAIL

After one of his customary virtual strolls around his old neighborhood in the Thereafter, the alien who so arbitrarily fills these pages consults his mailbox and selects the messages that best fit his obsessive, somewhat haywire frame of mind.

> After our profitable sales of water from Lourdes, nine-pronged Hebrew candelabra made in China, and prayer mats with in-built compasses, we have decided to promote an original, most serviceable new idea in respect of the burkas worn by the hallowed women of Afghanistan. Our company has patented a model of garment that filters the substances introduced into the air by pollution and eliminates their viruses and germs according to the latest international standard. This offer of feminine

ecological garb could be successfully marketed in the potent, newly emerging Asian markets and the macro-cities of Europe that have fallen victim to climate change and the disasters provoked by global warming.

(Signed: "Alice")

It is vital to guilt-trip the subject selected for the operation. And make him understand his responsibility in carrying out our just sentence that brooks no appeal. The fact that his very existence constitutes an obstacle to our grand project of social and ideological renewal and identity construction. The moral imperative to strengthen the Organization and end once and for all the suffering of the People allows no exceptions: it is a nonnegotiable right. Those who would disregard this and continue their daily, supposedly harmless activities, selfishly cocooned in labor and family spaces, are accomplices in this corrupt, nominal democracy in which they frolic and delight. Any person unaffiliated with the program of the Commandos for the Liberation of the Classes Oppressed by the System runs the risk of becoming a military target. Whether they be the beautiful people, the bosses, servants of the Puppet State, or suspicious types like you. The Organization keeps a close eye on your movements and can identify you whatever your disguise is. Quite unawares, fool, you may find yourself targeted by our strategy. Remember that, idiot: to warn is not to betray.

(Signed: the Crack Revenue Inspector)

Day in day out we see your twisted visage on your web page as if you haven't a friend in the world. Don't yield to decrepitude and despondency. Get in sync with your dreams. If you aren't happy with yourself and that face you see in your mirror, contact us right away. Our computer graphics whizzes will design you a genuinely natural smile.

(Signed: L'Oréal)

INTERCULTURAL DIALOGUE

What *is* the difference between the plaits of an ultra-orthodox Jew from Brooklyn and the dreadlocks of a Rasta rapper from Jamaica? Our hero consults various Biblical exegeses and the stocks of a CD store in the barrio he roamed when alive, and can come to no conclusion. Nonetheless, a little ray of light crosses his pitiful brain, worn out by so many and such futile enquiries.

The cap, the black or crochet hats that top them and underline their charismatic role!

He dashes into an Afro hair stylist and, a few streets down, completes his look in a milliner's adjacent to a well-known kosher restaurant. Wearing his rabbi (or rapper-touched-by-Grace) outfit, he decides to attend an intercultural symposium set up by distinguished representatives of the three religions of the Book. The center sponsoring it is only a few yards from the boulevard in question, and, preening himself with the dignity afforded by his attire (black on black after carefully dyeing his clothes at a dry cleaners), he stalks into the assembly hall and sits down in the first row in the stalls.

"Alice," turbaned, with hennaed beard, as on her web page, winks at him, indicating he should come onto the dais and participate in the colloquium advertised on the Internet. Next to her he spots Monsignor, the beloved of Christ via Young Boys, whose porno messages clog up his inbox daily.

What's the subject under debate? He doesn't know and it's an idle question. The hall has been emptied by a bomb threat: the drunken beggar who peered in for a few moments, spat on the floor, and lurched out to a chorus of insults and V-signs. Will they exchange spam or praise the exalted nature of their respective religions? "Alice" kicks off. Our grotesque rabbi's hopes of hearing her promote the model of burka destined to protect its wearers from the polluted environment are dashed. The radical imam lowers her voice and invites them to raise a hand to their earlobes. Thanks to a triple agent from the Chechen-slaughtering Czar's Intelligence Services, the CIA, and the Commandos for the Liberation of the Oppressed Classes, he has found the way to produce polonium 2010 at home! Monsignor prefers to speak about his missionary work proselytizing in Thailand. Our fainthearted hero remains silent: hidden security cameras are filming the proceedings. Out in the street, a contingent of police protects the symposium orators from a group of hostile demonstrators waving banners and shouting slogans against immigrants and their insidious fifth column: the esoteric intercultural dialogue!

HONOR, RACE, BLOOD, AND FIDELITY

The National Radical Party offers an electoral program as clear as it is efficient, to oppose the appeasing, limp-wristed policies of our rivals across the whole political spectrum. There are no social classes in our unique matrix: only pathogenic agents. A dusky-skinned fifth column is dangerously proliferating a species of half-breeds. Christian Europe cannot simply stand by and watch herself be swamped. Whiteness or death! The sun on our beaches is our enemy number one!

(Our mutant protagonist, the Monster of Le Sentier, Rasta rabbi, "Alice," thinks she catches a glimpse of her former neighbor from those distant days when she owned that flat in the Thereafter, and of the Madrid taxi-driver in whose vehicle she was trapped during a traffic jam in the course of a virtual journey of which we have no record.)

HUMAN RIGHTS!

No need to tell me, buddy! As if I didn't know them like the back of my hand! All friendly smiles and the second you're not watching, a knife in yer back! They only know how to obey and cower under the whip, like in their own lands. They pretend to work their butt off and, the moment you take yer eyes off them, they're backsliding. All they can think about is knocking back and sleeping, the motherfuckers! You only have to see them eating their pot of couscous with both hands and they'd use three if they had three! You can take it from me they have no manners or hygiene. Their shacks are real pigsties. They complain about the lack of running water, but why do they need it? "Clean" is an obscene word as far as they're concerned. Get a whiff of their filthy, stinking camps and squares! My father, RIP, was a colonel in the Legion and he warned me: don't ever trust them, hit them hard and they'll respect you! And now these stuck-up legal types come and tell you about their laws and nitpicking twaddle. I'd like to see them live next door to them for a couple of weeks. And these damned associations that reckon they're full of solidarity are to blame for all this stupidity. Who's pulling the wool over whose eyes? Their crap about human rights is filling our country with whores, muggers, and tramps! And what's more their women expect to give birth in our hospitals on the taxpayer's dime. How'd we ever get into this state!

STELLAR PORN

"Alice" carefully secretes her secrets away. His vocation as a triple agent requires a continuous rotation of roles that test her intellect and skills. The concealment tactics recommended by her bosses ratify behavior that is a hundred percent opposed to their precepts. She smokes, drinks, dabbles in drugs, and struts her stuff in nightclubs in shows with a dubious moral content. When he heard about that, our hero slipped in among the customers of a famous club frequented by the beautiful people. Inside, separated from the public and surrounded in the darkness by a bubble of light, "Alice" performs a sketch inspired by Félicien Rops. Wearing gloves, stockings, and thigh-length boots, shaking a lurid mop of hair, she walks naked along the catwalk while she ties up a pig with her belt and proudly plays the role of a porn star. The slavering clientele masturbate or feel up the girls at their table. "Alice's" scorn and pride are on red alert. The bourgeois she hates dream of being let into her dressing room, of getting an eyeful of his wondrously rotund breasts, bulging belly, magical navel, and blossoming pubis.

After such a display, who would ever suspect "her"—or "him," for that matter—of contacts with Monsignor Lover of Children and the rabbi with the hat and Rasta dreadlocks? or of her dual existence as the imam with the hennaed beard haranguing, scolding, railing against the existing order and inciting the faithful to join his holy crusade?

Nobody, absolutely nobody, despite the cooperation between several secret services in the war being waged against terrorism. Our protagonist is in the know and has recourse to a coded language when communicating with her. They meet in the dressing rooms of the cabaret where "Alice" performs his porno acts and they enjoy a sibylline, allusive, knowing conversation.

"Thirteen is no longer thirteen. Take away two."

"As in . . ."

"Shut up! He who remains silent, speaks!"

"I only wanted to . . ."

"I meant what I said! Back to your computer and wait for my orders."

The Monster feels like a fish out of water and doesn't know where he is: whether he's in the nightclub with the beautiful people or in the Hereafter checking out his e-mails.

"ALICE" IN PARISIAN WONDERLAND

In order to put the agents of the different secret services that are after her off her trail, "Alice" avoids the hustle and bustle of the ethnic neighborhoods that so attract our deceased protagonist. She flaunts her charms along the great clean and tidy avenues bustling with elegantly dressed tourists or natives exuding unmistakable cachet. She swans down the Champs-Elysées like a queen, in a broad-brimmed straw hat or an eye-catching feathery concoction, stops and stares at the Vuitton and Armani window displays and ogles at the businessman leaving his chauffeured limousine to rush to a date on the terrace at Fouquet's. When she reaches Rond-Point she reacts as in apparent ecstasy to the noble lines of the surrounding buildings, films them on her video camera, and retraces her steps to the Arc de Triomphe.

If she can change her destiny, she'll opt for an artistic, literary pedigree. He sits down in Les Deux Magots and looks entranced at the nearby church. He's a couple of seconds from Sartre's place, heads down the Rue Saint-Benoît to say hello to la Duras, flits over to the Rue Schoelcher to exchange a few words with Simone, and pounds down Vaneau on the lookout for Gide's old pad. His cultural concerns, dress, and behavior quash any suspicion she belongs to some clandestine organization. She follows the Stations of the Cross on the adoration of the great and the good and engages in multilingual dialogue with both visitors and natives. Yes, the boulevard you want is the second on the right. Her Paris is Hemingway's, not that of the radical Islamists or Anti-System Commandos who preach its destruction.

PROMISES OF SALVATION

Who wouldn't be driven mad if all around is but oppression, rabble-rousing, and deceit, tenements where rubbish piles up and shantytowns isolated from the outside world while you can see the shameless opulence of the beautiful people on television, in magazines, and the other brutalizing media that perpetuate the stupidity of the People?

Had they been born for this, and only for this? To wander like stray dogs, to grow up uneducated, joining gangs, submitting to the rule of the strongest and the dialectic of clenched fists, handing joints around and trading in hashish? Spending time in revolting jails and coming out resolved to get their revenge for being so shamed and humiliated?

The image of the bearded guy on his web page, accompanied by clips of wars and military training, cement walls around defenseless ghettos, exploding car bombs and ritual farewells, is like a shaft of light penetrating the dismal gloom of their lives.

The mysterious imam so lavish with his advice promises to lead them along the path of righteousness and drag them out of the quagmire where they are sinking, offers the possibility of redemption, of scaling heroic heights, of brandishing a humble sword against killers and executioners, of sacrificing themselves with a belt full of explosives in the teeth of the upholders of the System responsible for their unhappiness.

In one of his rare moments of lucidity, the deceased flâneur of Le Sentier gazes at "Alice" and becomes increasingly anxious. Ever since he entered the Hereafter (that infinite computer center from where his lurid e-mails help us to write this book), he hasn't seen any of those sacrificed for the cause she argues for on his web site getting anywhere near their glorious promised destiny.

WE'LL MAKE SURE THEY TAKE NOTICE OF YOU

You just have to accept that your life has been a washout. Tedious work, impossible loves, endless disappointments. You dreamed of a brilliant career: spurting out of the sludge like a geyser, giving yourself all the elements of a winner. You wanted to be renowned and admired like a film star or ace footballer. Pose for photographers, sign autographs, and appear on TV and in women's magazines. But you've sunk unfailingly into routine mediocrity. Nobody mentions your name or greets you in the street. You are a total nonentity.

We can rescue you from this dark pit and guarantee you a few moments of glory as an incredible celebrity. An estimated audience of over ten million viewers fascinated and captivated by the heavenly climax to your life. How often have you thought of committing suicide, even though you knew such an end would go unnoticed, and indeed confirm your total insignificance in the world's spotlights! All you have to do is contact us and follow our instructions to the letter, and your dreams will come true. The exclusive opportunity we're offering will appeal to the media's need to break news and redeem you from all those gray years when you were ground down to no avail by rancorous envy and frustration.

Our secure links with various armed groups in the most bellicose regions on the planet enable us to put our trust—in the safest, most discreet circumstances—in people like you, who aspire to penetrate the hearts and homes of millions and millions and communicate directly with that huge mass of men and women who will hold their breath as they watch the scene in which YOU will be the lead actor. Like a sublime character created by Shakespeare, you will clamor that you are innocent before the cameras, will entreat, will sob, and will perhaps even succeed in softening the flinty hearts of your captors: you will get a pardon. Or else, conversely, a consummate professional in the field will decapitate you in a matter of seconds, in the slickest of performances. Hair-raising, you will say: but what do these few seconds of terror matter compared with the universal consecration we will bring you? A simple e-mail with your personal details can propel you to heights of fame you could never have attained on your own! Go for the spotlights on the catwalks of the stars! Our multi-service branches guarantee a swift transition to the notoriety you so covet!

DANGEROUS LIAISONS

The lives of "Alice" and our deceased in his brief and unfortunate incursions into the Thereafter are shot through with innumerable patches of shadows that are thick, opaque, and quite impenetrable. What does *she* do, for example, when she repairs to one of her safe conspiratorial places, after a round of fiery preaching or an acclaimed performance as a porn diva? Does he select protean, variegated disguises from her wardrobe or zealously surrender to the daily rituals of prayer? Does she live alone or surrounded by disciples ripe for self-immolation, as soon as he orders it, in the name of their Maker?

Idle questions, since a radical activist like her doesn't let up for a moment. Donning her chieftain's turban and bushy beard she contacts, through web pages with constantly changing passwords, other militant radicals with inflexibly Messianic convictions: Talibans, Etarras, avengers of Masada, and Legionaries from the Bishops' Conference. Thanks to help from an experienced hacker—a profession equally rated in the Hereafter!—the deceased witnesses her exchange of messages with the rabbi sporting the black cap and Rasta dreadlocks who has boldly mounted the platform where the interfaith dialogue in support of peace and tolerance the reader finds so very familiar was in full swing.

"My very dear enemy!"

"Soul sister!"

"Our strategies match, do they not?"

"Right on they do!"

"The worse it gets, the better!"

"Extremes touch."

"Your extremes are most touching."

"Yes, we are touching."

"My hand's got a feel!"

"Mine's got a good grip too!"

The Monster hopes to melt into an embrace, perhaps the most private of all feels. But cyberspace intervenes and he's left wanting it, but not before his now wrinkled, useless knob, relishing a festive semi-erection, is treated to a tingle.

NO, YOU'RE ON THE WRONG TRACK

He should start firearm training in order to fight the System's kill-ers and what better place to do so than at a shooting association, the haunt of the beautiful people in their leisure time?

"Alice" had found him some designer clothes she'd bought in the hunting and fishing section of a department store on the Champs-Elysées and, after hiring a chauffeur-driven limousine of the kind used by rich celebrities, she escorted him wearing her broad-brimmed straw hat and grand dame outfit to an exclusive club (or so its publicity claimed) situated in the city's residential outskirts. She was carrying membership cards, with aristocratic monikers, linked (or so she claimed) to dethroned royalty and, af-ter ordering a double scotch from the waiter, she soon found a seat on the terrace at that deserted hour from where she could watch and weigh up the apprenticeship of our book's elated hero. The use of firearms had become a repeated theme in his dreams from the day he'd returned to his lair in the Thereafter via cyberspace!

As the reader will have surmised, the training session was a disaster. The aspiring terrorist lacked the necessary reflexes, missed the target time and again, couldn't pick up the tricks of the trade, not by a long shot. The bang-bangs from his official police pistol resounded with an exhausting regularity, while "Alice's" irritated scowl deepened in proportion to his flops and transformed into a scornful leer. Her queenly airs didn't allow her to stoop to insulting him, or, more justifiably, to shooting him with her CETME. She retained her surface calm and, when reapplying eyeliner to her lashes with the help of his small mirror, she reached the inevitable conclusion: rather than weaponry suited to the elite of the Anti-System Commandos, a clumsy militant like him needed a belt full of explosives like those worn by the guys who self-immolate in order to attain the power and the glory in the other life that they'd failed miserably to get anywhere near on this side of the divide.

OF GOURMETS AND FUNDAMENTALISTS

If hypocrisy is the homage vice pays to virtue, provocation must be its symmetrical opposite. Our readers know that only too well: "Alice," who performs her stellar porno act in the sinful dive of that disco, turns out to be a man of profound religious convictions and strict regimentation in his private life. He hennas daily every single hair of his beard with the same drive for perfection as the odious rabbi knots his dreadlocks. As for Monsignor, the beloved of Jesus Christ, he combines ethereal love with a playful predilection for children. He mistakenly believes that our deceased hero shares his tastes, unaware that the Swedish professor has demonstrated in her thesis that the real object of his desires were mustachioed immigrants who flaunted and touted it in cinemas and bathrooms.

The three seers refine and perfect the secret piety of their lives with practices that apparently belie it. From time to time, they meet in the Prelature to which they gain entry via a secret door, after whispering the password to the sentinel. The central character from these pages attends their councils in the capacity of a guest statue. He keeps quiet and listens attentively to their theological-scientific disquisitions on the intelligent design of the universe and the tortuous roads to salvation. Sometimes, those present—the rabbi sent his apologies today because it is the Sabbath—chat about the worldliest of matters, like the fondness they share for good food.

A famous Cordon Bleu, official provider to the Curia, has thought up a menu for them that he e-mailed a few minutes ago to the Monsignor's account and which we reproduce verbatim:

> Entrée: a Roman salad.
> First course: Camerlengo with a *parfum* of white smoke.
> Second course: St Peter's steak (rare) in purple sauce.
> Desserts: Nun's finger dipped in Benedictine.

("Alice" is licking her lips and Monsignor is laughing with the would-be innocence of a little boy. Only the deceased abstains: the dead don't eat. His material self vanished into nothingness on the wretched day he left his lair in the Thereafter.)

WHAT'S A MONSIGNOR LIKE
YOU DOING IN A BOOK LIKE THIS?

The Beloved of Jesus Christ via Little Boys doesn't approve of having recourse to violence like "Alice" and the Rasta rabbi. In line with the norms of the Bishops' Conference and that infallible deprogrammer of Limbo, *alias* Benedict the Antiquated, he defends the Family, the Holy Family of male and female, that procreator of children. The pill, condoms, legal abortion, and marriage between people of the same sex hinder the healthy propagation of the species, the natural multiplying of the young things he dedicates all his love and energy to. Following instructions from on high, he eulogizes an agreement drawn up on that theme with representatives of other faiths in the teeth of opposition from the coarse rabble of disbelievers and secularists: the Family as the foundation of religious, political, and social power.

Resplendent with cope and bewitching miter, Monsignor tours the world like a broody hen protecting her hatch beneath a plump rump. "Alice" and their other partners in interfaith dialogue uphold his healthy principles: we need soldiers and caudillos, fertile women and legions of little angels to secure the continuation of the species! His missions extend from Southeast Asia to sub-Saharan Africa, from the Mayan Coast to Tahiti. The press lauds them and compares him to Mother Teresa. He gives interviews to CNN, *Vogue*, and *Paris Match*.

But it's one big front and the deceased Monster knows this better than anyone. Monsignor floods his mailbox with e-mails profusely illustrated with photographs of his protégés in seraphic poses grinning cheekily childish grins.

"What do think about number twenty-six? My acolyte brings him to my bedroom to warm my sheets and he's great fun.

"The twins aren't bad either, don't you think? I play their flutes and they seem very happy and genuinely celestial.

"Oh, how vast the harvest and how few the reapers!"

Our little dwarf (which is what we all are, seen from the Hereafter) keeps asking about the seemingly intelligent design of the universe (whether it could be a simple illusion of the senses, and whether there might be *nothing* out there, rather than something). His experience in both worlds strengthens his innate skepticism: the suspicious mind of the poor in spirit or of a schizoid towards shepherds of the flock.

YOU'RE ALWAYS PIGGY IN THE MIDDLE

"Alice" had sent him to the rioting suburbs: to the fertile terrain for recruiting volunteers prepared to commit to action. As night fell he reached the devastated parks where those guys gathered far from the strident sirens of ambulances and police. As he managed to glean from a distance, they talked to each other in a *lingua franca* concocted from African, Basque, Arabic, and Urdu dialects. Thanks to their multi-use cell phones they sent reports to half the globe and received back new orders and slogans. They exchanged roles and roll-ups. Some injected heroin into their forearms. Others prayed dutifully or surrendered to animist rites and invoked Changó and Yemayá. He also noted the presence of the pigs, of cops disguised as Tom, Dick, or Harry, searching for material evidence of a bomb factory. They'd discovered a suspicious-looking bottle, the label of which sent them into ecstasy. The forensic scientist accompanying them immediately proceeded to an examination and declared that the label was a luggage-locker ticket, somewhat discolored by the effects of bad weather. It was boric acid! "An explosive?" asked our busybody. "Well, one possible ingredient," replied the scientific cop. Or do you fall for the yarn they spin that it's only used for killing roaches? As if we didn't know this crew couldn't care a fig about hygiene?

The information from the bottle flowed like a river into an ocean of hypotheses. Who'd left it there? Did it point to the existence of a secret plan to commit terrorist attacks? Or was it a ploy to divert the cops' investigation from the right path? Such conjectures danced round their heads when they spotted a bearded fellow in a thicket bordering on the object of their ruminations, apparently engrossed in theological, nay, perhaps terrorist speculations. Could it be "Alice" himself? Our deceased mutant began to shake. What would happen if they pounced on him and, under pressure from questioning—as the police services would euphemistically report—she confessed what she must confess. Let's say it loud and clear and expose the fellow's moral fiber: he wanted to clear off in one foul swoop to his Hereafter, but the bastard law of gravity prevented him from so doing. His fears weren't realized, fortunately for him. The pigs merely photographed beardy with his cell phones as he disappeared into the distance looking for a cybercafé.

FROM THE REPUBLIC TO THE BASTILLE

"Alice's" long-term strategy is variously phased. The first, and mother to the rest, depends on securing resources and partners in the big charity business. It's all about reaching the hearts of citizens, attracted, she titters to the deceased, by the Thrust of an Ideal. About recruiting to the ranks of the Pro-Peace and Tolerance Association thousands of altruistic, solidarity militants ("idiot assholes," she calls them) alert to its declared objective: the raising of funds to help the abandoned children in the Third World (the photo of a smiling Monsignor figures prominently in its messages and publicity ads, a Monsignor surrounded by happy kids on one of his pastoral tours of Thailand!), funds which would then be diverted to phantom stakeholders, specializing in the invention and creation of projects: the purchase and sale of shares in high-risk groups, the juicy profits from which will be spent acquiring a wide range of weapons, and on the ideological and religious indoctrination of youths excluded from the System or victims of the oppressive State.

Thanks to these charitable souls, "Alice" confides, the machine of subversion whirs into action, and, as he hears these words, the character whose wanderings we are following as best we can in the pages you cannot put down (allergic to any good works after his harsh experience in the Hereafter) feels like a shrimp or mollusk in water. Just take a look at him, dear reader, participating with such airs in the big annual march the association organizes through the capital's boulevards. He's wearing a wristband with the Monsignor's logo and slips among the Third World militants, catching celebrities on his video camera and bawling out slogans until he goes hoarse. Now he's linking arms with brawny spokesmen for a group with a strange acronym. But don't think he's up to no good: for once you'll be wrong. He's not trying to pick anyone up; rather he's whispering the password that identifies him as a double agent. According to orders from on high, they must take advantage of the non-aggressive nature of the act and the puny police contingent to change the slogans and aims agreed upon and the small band of the initiated must embark on their preplanned surprise guerrilla action: smash shop windows, burn cars, and up-end garbage cans.

Who says that May '68 is dead? There he is, the mere thirty-seven-year-old of yesteryear, hurling paving stones and erecting barricades against the System's killers, garlanded by a charming, romantic halo. In line with the ubiquity and anachronism feeding this narrative, he spots his former comrades from their various revolutionary groups, new philosophers to boot, and imagines himself leading the assault on some hateful Bastille. He looks in vain for "Alice" among the protagonists of that festive fraternity. The little innocent doesn't realize he's got the wrong era and that the person pulling the strings is not moved by ephemeral contingency. Dressed as a diva, his mentor is following the virtual event on TV and sending e-mails to her partners before rushing to the nightly performance of her much-lauded porn act in that nightclub.

MISSION ASSIGNED

A messenger has brought a packet containing an explosives belt to his old apartment in the Thereafter. The package includes a leaflet with instructions on how to put it together, hide, and detonate it. It's pointless saying the hapless fellow doesn't understand a word and wastes precious time obstinately and futilely trying to memorize these instructions. Tired by all this exertion, he plonks himself in front of the mirror and tries to attach the weapon to his belt. The full-length view of himself and the device is disheartening. The package is visible under his shirt and makes him look pregnant. For a moment he wonders whether he should disguise himself in the flowing robes of his next-door neighbor, but decides against. How could he ever find the wig, the mink, and the high heels? He decides to buy a hunting jacket from the branch of a well-known sportswear store, tries his size in several models and opts to round off his purchases with a peaked cap and Bermuda shorts that give him a burlesque air. But also turn him into an ingenuous, gawping sort of guy.

Protected by his flashy, brand-new clothes, smile courtesy of L'Oréal, our budding human bomb walks the streets without arousing suspicions. He goes into the nearby market, takes the metro, changes line several times, peers out at the bourgeois districts inhabited by the class enemy and works out a list of eventual targets. The orders from on high are precise, but leave an ample margin of freedom. Why this place and not that? Why one day and not another? He is proud of his ability to make decisions. The lives of hundreds of individuals depend on him! He puffs out his chest under his death-sowing vest and his customary timorous gait gives way to a ridiculous, exaggerated military strut!

PERAMBULATION INTERRUPTUS

"Excuse me, but aren't you my neighbor from number 33?"

A svelte lady, with a vaguely familiar face, smiles and holds out a hand to our tourist in disguise.

"I had heard you'd passed away, but I see it's not true. There's nothing so strange as life! One's here, one disappears, and one pops up again! Isn't it all rather extraordinary?"

The man wearing the explosives belt has no choice but to agree.

"Yes, indeed it is."

"They once gave me up for dead and here you see me as fresh as a cucumber! People get bored and talk for talk's sake. The important thing is to have a clear goal in life, don't you think?"

"I think so."

"I have one, you have one, but I don't know what yours is."

"Is that a question . . . ?"

"Yes, I was going to my aerobics class, suddenly saw you, and concluded that my fate depended on yours."

"Can you tell me why?"

"I don't know and that's precisely why I'm asking *you*."

"If you don't mind . . . How should I put this? I feel your question is rather *intrusive*."

"That is in the very nature of a question."

"Madame . . ."

"Don't go! I dreamed about you last night and do you know what my dream was?"

"How could I?"

"I was following in the footsteps of a terrorist. He was dressed like you and was wearing an explosives belt!"

"You are quite mistaken, Madame."

"No, I am not. *I* sent you the weapons via a messenger service!"

Our wretched hero shudders, his brow dripping with sweat. She looks at him contemptuously and abruptly flashes at him her counterespionage credentials and membership card in her country's secret services.

"Don't let this business go to your head! You've got to be humble, patient and follow the orders you get from 'Alice' to the letter!"

THE CONSPIRACY

Engrossed in the contemplation of a print of St. Anthony tenderly embracing a child (whose little butt he's supporting with a bound copy of a manual of piety), Monsignor was in no rush to reach the Hereafter. He was happy enough in the Thereafter. He was sponsoring educational projects for homeless children in Thailand and other countries God seemed to have forgotten. He'd joined an agency specializing in Journeys of a Lifetime and was flying from one continent to another, sewing the seeds of his mission. His bedside reading was the Kempis by the Saint Escrivá of Barbastro, and he kept rereading his maxims.

Why glide weightlessly between seraphim and archangels, if love for children on this microscopic sinful planet of ours enables us to refine our merits and virtues and brings greater profit and satisfaction? he asked our usual suspect when they were heading to one of the preparatory meetings for the Pro-Peace and Tolerance dialogue, the strings of which our "Alice" pulled.

The anxious hero of these pages nodded silently. This meeting with the hennaed bearded fundamentalist preacher didn't make the least sense. The agenda for the assembly, as posted on the Internet, spoke of mutual understanding, common values, and open cultures: tomfoolery from the most obtuse, the lamest leftists, tittered the organizer. Indeed, the politically correct program was at total, yes, total variance with what had been secretly planned by those summoned to the old building in a Le Sentier backstreet. As they puffed their way up the staircase to the attic, the two characters bumped into members of the Commandos for the Liberation of the Classes Oppressed by the System, the Martyrs of Al-Andalus, unreconstructed Maoists, and other groups making their way to their respective destinations, carrying the requisite indoctrination on board. Nobody said a word upstairs. The conspirators knew the rules of the game: cell phones switched off, exchange of coded messages immediately reduced to ash by cigarette lighters, the gestures and expressions of militants skilled in clandestine practices. Despite all his puerile attempts to fathom the situation, the old local understood zilch. What *was* the point of the meeting? He scrutinized conspiratorial lip movements and knowing winks in vain. No one seemed to heed his insignificant presence and not even we ourselves could help. An unknown virus has infected the computers in the limbo from which we are constructing this scene!

At the end of the conclave, those present left the conference table and nodded farewell to each other. The Monster was left alone with an "Alice" in ecstatic epiphany. Their plans were looking good! What was at stake, she scribbled on a scrap of paper she immediately destroyed, were the necessary preliminaries for the execution of a bomb attack against a building that was quite emblema . . .

EMBLEMATIC!

How can we describe the violent wave of aversion that coursed through our veins? We had estimated fines of a thousand euros for the use of *that* word and solid prison sentences for backsliders, but "Alice" of the thousand faces still snuck it past us! Do forgive us, dear reader, we beg you. Albeit downheartedly, we shall ask our editor to suppress that nasty word to avoid any aftereffects from its pollution, as devastating as any from those pesticides used by the fruit and horticultural industry that saturate the supermarkets where our main character bought his supplies when he was still alive, being such a routinely apathetic, irremediably shortsighted guy.

NEVER BE WHERE YOU OUGHT NOT TO BE

Never in airport terminals for domestic flights or otherwise, whether within the Community or the rest of the world. On metro lines, trains, or buses, however safe you think they are. In cafés, nightclubs, and other such nocturnal dives. In offices, workshops, factories, and other workplaces. Certainly not in administrative buildings, banks, and hospitals that are usually so jam-packed. Nor in stadiums, rap concerts, or locations tourist agencies include in their itineraries. Rush hours and city bottlenecks are particularly dangerous. Keep clear of elevators, skyscrapers, department stores, and underground parking lots.

Above all, never stay at home leafing through the newspapers, watching TV or fucking your better half. He will always be our main strategic target.

POLONIUM 2010

He was recently moved, in his asleep, to the spiral stairs of a newly built airport parking lot. Somebody (he didn't manage to see who) gave him the suitcase and carry-on and pointed to the elevator to the exit level. He went up alone, didn't press a single button, and, ascent completed, he dragged his bags to the long moving belt that negotiated him slowly through the metal and glass entrails of a universe of design engineering in which he was the only living being. He could see rising platforms, escalators, and endless passageways. Nobody and nothing broke the astonishing silence. He moved forward, ever forward, never alighting from his mobile carpet disappearing into the distance and into time. He eyed abandoned carts, ownerless valises and backpacks, and sank into a state of diffuse panic. He followed the direction signs under a huge vault where the sky was visible. When he reached the forlorn check-in hall, he looked on the screen for the company that had issued him his ticket. Its staff had vanished as well, but he found the boarding card an employee had clearly earmarked for him before she beat it. When he placed his suitcase on the check-in ramp, the latter automatically switched on. Faithfully following directions issued by electronic devices, he found airport security: a long, intestinal snake that twisted and turned and finally led to metal detection arches the police had inexplicably abandoned. The Gehenna described by Dante was a complex imbroglio of escalators and elevators, a little driverless clockwork train, a new upstairs and downstairs, deserted passport controls, warning signs aimed at no one. Cafés and duty-free shops were also frighteningly silent. The doors to the passenger boarding bridge remained shut. He looked in vain for an information desk. An ownerless poodle barked in commiseration. New Year's Greetings and special offers added a touch of black humor and Santa Claus smiled and slavered out of the corner of his lips and wet his fake beard. What had happened in this labyrinth normally stuffed with travelers in a frantic rush? He wandered like an immigrant without papers through that merciless void when a note hurriedly scrawled on the back of his boarding card, which he'd only just looked at, revealed the reason for the stampede out. It simply said: TOTAL QUARANTINE, PO-LONIUM 2010.

KEEP AN EYE OUT, BUDDY

Watch that tourist in a baseball cap and Bermudas taking a photo of the Eiffel Tower from the esplanade of the Trocadéro and looking such a fool. Well, not so. He may be "Alice." Or an imam from the Martyrs of Al-Andalus. Or a member of the Commands for the Liberation of the Oppressed Classes. Or an ETA-Leninist red beret. Or . . .

(The list of radical groups and gangs is a lengthy one. It wouldn't fit on this page, let alone in this whole book!)

All these portrait artists you can see are suspiciously filming targets related to future terrorist attacks and, as an elementary precaution, you should steer clear of them and warn the police, after checking, to be sure, that your cell phone hasn't been bugged.

But stop this idle speculation and follow him to the bus that will take him to the suburban train station where a mass of commuters whose degree of blackness skyrockets as they move away from the city's more select, well-heeled areas. He went into the Gentlemen's and came out of the Ladies'. You won't recognize his face but the kids in the gangs will, the ones that rule the roost in the decrepit apartment blocks where their parents were imprisoned. They are all on the friendliest terms with him, open a way up for him, act as bodyguards. He's the Horny Rapper, whose CDs with their incendiary lyrics circulate from hand to hand and call for rebellion against social exclusion and racist arrogance, denounce the slavery of neocolonialism and its corrupt puppet regimes, proclaiming that violence is a legitimate, political weapon. The Rapper hammers this home and much more besides: coded messages to kick off urban guerrilla warfare, instructions for making homemade explosives, basic rules for the establishment of sleeper cells that act independently of one another, thus rendering the police's task much more difficult in case there is a round up. His "Hundred-headed Hydra" and "Kill 'Em, Heaven Will Forgive You" are his big concert hits and have become the anthems unifying those who are taking on the System. The Rapper boasts he has magic powers superior to those of tyrants like Mobutu or Teodoro Obiang. He speaks of the Lord and his Swords of Fire, of the creed of the Born-Again Christians and the fatwas of the blind imam and obscure ayatollahs. He blasts away and sways his hips, parades regally on stage, gives the finger and blows kisses, cheered on by unswerving addicts to the struggle in the grip of preachers who promise justice on earth and limitless glory in the Hereafter.

THE RULES OF THE GAME

Throw the enemy into disarray with fictitious plans and decoy traps. Set him onto clues that lead nowhere. Sharpen the contradictions in the System. Open breaches in his defenses, slip through, extend them, and fight him from the inside.

The Manual for the Perfect Suicide passed on by "Alice" deeply perplexes our defunct hero. Any place, however small, can become a military objective. Any person ("You too!") can become the target for an attack. What matters is the impact on the media. Ensure there are cameras around to capture the moment of horror, thus allowing it to be transmitted commercially on the main TV channels at peak viewing times.

The downcast Monster reviews the pages of the manual and gleans its maxims in a desperate attempt to understand something.

Drain the water so the fish die.

Terror is absolute by its very nature and brooks no artificial limits.

Don't look for alibis, your task will always be an end in itself.

The sacred cause may vary, the act of destruction never does.

Stop pussyfooting and get a slice of the action!

"Alice" fans herself and smiles. Such diverse groups as The Lord's Army, The Virtuously Violent, Nostalgia for Stalin, and other bands opposed to the crimes of capitalism and the arrogance of its idols have just signed up for her secret, password-protected website!

POLICE COMMUNIQUÉ

After a period of observation and then of hot pursuit carried out in collaboration with Interpol, Security Headquarters can announce the arrest of a dangerous group of radicals who were preparing to launch several terrorist attacks on public buildings and means of transport. Thanks to inside information from a double agent, it was decided to follow closely upon the (high) heels of an imam whose apparently moderate and open sermons were a cover for activities to recruit teenagers and youths from districts with a record of conflict, ready to go into action and commit suicide attacks. The abode of the gang's leader was searched and military training videos were discovered along with computer software, timers, bomb-making manuals, and other lethal weapons: plastic explosives, Titadine,

DNT, nitroglycerine, sarin gas, and polonium 2010. The terrorists' plans were still at a preparatory phase, following a medium-term strategy of action. The capture operation was carried out simultaneously in various locations in the city and areas on the periphery. Those arrested offered no resistance and have been placed at the disposition of the courts: Imam Abu Emzauer, and five minors responding to the respective initials of M. A., A. B., H. H., K. B., and R. D. The Prefect of Police has sent a message congratulating the head of security forces, and all officers and agents, for the rapid and efficient nature of their intervention.

THE BALL IS IN THE COURT OF THE SMARTASSES

Don't worry, dear reader. The narrative puzzle doesn't fizzle out here. The people under arrest aren't who you think they are. Or, anyway, the people the police crow about in their pompous official communiqué.

Before moving on to the operational stage of their plot, "Alice" and her accomplices took the elementary precaution of training a number of stand-ins to play their various roles. They sought out selfless, stupid militants (illiterates raised in poverty-stricken barrios) ready to sacrifice themselves for the good of the cause: with a view to an inevitably crooked trial in which deft, well-paid lawyers would demolish one by one the pieces of evidence brought forth by the intelligence services and the arguments put forward by the public prosecutor. The publicity would do them no harm whatsoever. After a few weeks, the daily broadcasting of the trial would rescue them from anonymity and give them an enviable visibility. And all that without taking into account their divine reward: eternal paradise with their pick of virgins and little children, morsels to suit everyone's taste. The real conspirators celebrated the success of their ruse in a well-known beer-cellar near Le Sentier. A *halal* menu with all the sophistication of a Michelin three-starrer. When it came to desserts, they raised their champagne flutes to the short-term victory of their strategy. Then "Alice" went to get ready for her nightly performance in the nightclub, and after bidding farewell to Monsignor and the other extremists, the bewildered hero of these pages started to pound more shoe leather around his old haunts, immersed in memories of past pickups and skirmishes with vanished colleagues in the Thereafter. He reflected on the peculiar nature of his fate, and, unaware of the privileges granted him by his status as the living dead (or death warmed up), he tried in vain to tie up the loose ends. Was he? Had he ever been? Would he be once more? As he stared at the ground while roaming in the gloaming, he came across an envelope addressed to himself in front of the post office, which he opened warily (lest it be a letter bomb!), and found it contained proposals for the redemption of society signed by the same Imam Abu Emzauer mentioned in the Security Headquarters communiqué.

"OPERATION SILENCE"

The psychological factor is vital in the holy war against the System and its big shots. In line with the orders from the Global Command uniting our brethren across the whole planet, you must contribute individually to the creation of a general atmosphere of anguish that will gradually turn into panic. How? It's very easy! Leave a suitcase or suspicious package in an airport terminal or metro station, or double-park a transit van with a false license plate, preferably next to an educational center or government building. The police's bomb disposal unit will soon find them and detonate them from a distance. The evacuation measures and then the noise from the explosions will upset tens of thousands of individuals who, at the beginning of this first phase of our operation, will breath a sigh of relief that there are no casualties, and that nothing is really amiss. But the daily repetition of the maneuver (cunningly abandoned packages, cases, and vans) and their subsequent detonation by remote control will finally create a sense of routine. Pedestrians, public transport users and all travelers will adapt and even feel comforted by the preventive measures enforced by the police chiefs and the on-the-spot diligence of their men. These soothing explosions should occur over a minimum period of three months until they become assimilated into citizens' everyday lives as something completely normal.

This first phase in our ascent to war will be followed by a silent stage. There will be no parcels, bags, or vehicles whose peculiar nature and vaguely scorched smell might prompt fear. A silence of this kind, rather than calming the populace, will give rise to a feeling of anguish. What are the police doing? Why have they dropped their guard and why are they leaving us at the mercy of the terrorists? Discontent will spread, provoked by opposition parties, and demonstrations will take place spontaneously against the newly exposed plight of the potential victims of our righteous cause. The psychologists advising us from the most prestigious US universities have dubbed this the "Silence Syndrome." Those affected can't stand the situation and live in a state of permanent anxiety, hoping for the next explosion or chain of explosions that will pacify them and confirm the swift, efficient intervention of the forces of law and order. There will be general relief on the day there are fresh explosions. There will be ubiquitous applause and shouts of joy until the moment comes when the mail, their cell phones, and the news media spread the terrible news—this was a genuine terrorist attack!

BUSINESS IS BUSINESS

In order to maintain the supply of economic resources to Anti-System combatants, we can and must have recourse to every means possible, however illegal and inhuman they may seem at first sight. To extortion, armed robbery, the execution of individuals completely in the thrall of capitalism or, if you prefer, of Big Satan. Our *brigadistas* for the holy cause have earned the right to enjoy the comforts of the liberated, under the peaceful cover of legality.

To this end, thanks to a well-conceived qualitative leap, we have proceeded to distribute material polluting babies' bottles, toothpaste, facial creams, and sweet-smelling aerosols, aided and abetted by unscrupulous manufacturers in the Third World and the transnational corporations whose well-known labels we hijack.

This ploy works like clockwork. The social alarm created when these products are discovered in stores by the health authorities in advanced societies justifies and indeed causes a rush on the anti-toxic brands sold by our partners, guaranteed (evidently at a much higher price) to entirely neutralize the poisons.

You don't believe me, ingenuous reader? Well switch on your television set right now or connect your cell to your favorite channel or program, and there you will see the renowned Horny Rapper in the thick of an advertising campaign for a lipstick, anti-wrinkle cream, or baby milk without noxious substances, to the tune of your favorite song, chorused by a mob of fans swaying and howling against a background curtain decorated with the slogan: YOUR HEALTH WILL ALWAYS BE OUR PRIMARY CONCERN.

NOTIONS OF LOGIC

In order to rebuild, destruction is indispensable. To clean the air we breathe daily, we must previously have polluted it. To sell ecological products, we must first infect the world with new species of virus and bacteria.

"Alice" and her peers with their different creeds and ideologies have understood this better than anyone and coordinate their terrorist activities with the transnationals of the sector that is supposedly affected. The explosion and resulting collapse of a barely profitable building planned by some developer who dreams of raising an emblematic building (that horrible word again!) over the bombsite. An avian or bovine plague at the precise moment a wide range of foodstuffs completely above suspicion is launched on the market. The poisoning of water reservoirs to coincide with the massive sale of diverse brands of table water with their respective, eloquent labels.

My dear reader, System and Anti-System complement each other! They work hand in glove and you haven't a clue! "Alice," with her mink coat and poodle (we've concealed her wardrobe and lapdog till now to avoid shocking you), rents a luxury suite in the Hilton and regularly chats to the politicians leading the anti-terrorist campaign (no need to mention names, you know who I mean!), as well as finance tycoons and arms manufacturers, seeking common ground and objectives. They argue about locations, dates, and media coverage for the next attacks. The war without concessions against terrorism requires the permanent reality of terror and its commercialization as a vital commodity. If you are reluctant to accept the truth or if you find the display of such cynicism too sickening, take a holiday on a paradisiacal island and relax in the sun by the poolside in a five-star hotel. Unfortunately for you, you won't know this place is going to be the target of a now-imminent lethal explosion destined to convince your recalcitrant travel agency of the justice and moral rectitude of our demands!

DON'T STICK YOUR NOSE IN
WHEN IT'S NONE OF YOUR BUSINESS

It would be futile to expect the deceased to undergo a modest apprenticeship in the principles and laws that rule the universe. His battered brain reels from one upset to another. Perhaps his continual journeys across stellar space have damaged his intellectual capacities. He feels as if he's being blown randomly about like a lowly, low-flying plastic bag. The seraphim and archangels he meets on the way pay him no damn attention. Coward that he is, he's terrified he will interfere with the flight of a ballistic missile from one of the defense shields that are proliferating on the woebegone planet. The wretch forgets he's dead: the war of the galaxies doesn't impact him! Even so, these and many other considerations in respect of the privileged immunity his status grants him don't spare him a helluva lot of stress when he considers the double mission "Alice" and his lieutenants in the Anti-System Commandos assigned him in the Le Sentier attic the reader is already familiar with. Not self-immolation in a market or bus station, but fanning the fires in shantytowns and conferring with some of those unbending leaders on southern shores who, in return for protection for their drug-laden biplanes and their safe arrival at their final destinations, will guarantee a fair distribution of the profits to the guerrilla movements and other radical groups unified under a single command: the millions and millions circulating, via murky bank transfers, to this poor world's fiscal paradises—antechamber, so Monsignor says, to those awaiting us in the Hereafter! But our hero has seen no sign of paradise: only a cyber park with thousands of computers. "Alice," mutant "Alice," is shuffling several packs and doesn't know which card to select. The line separating the System from the Anti-System fades before his very eyes. When he looks at himself and his bulletproof jacket, he doesn't know whether to laugh or to cry.

READ GENESIS, I BEG YOU

The Swedish professor hassles "Alice" with her e-mails. She's seen the deceased's posts on the pacifist association's website and demands information on the latter and the role the scribbler is playing there.

While she adds a touch of lipstick and another layer of mascara to her eyelashes, "Alice" sells her the usual goods with the professional expertise of a five-star PhD in the Business Sciences.

"We are promoting an ecumenical vision, get that, darling? Respect for difference and other people's values."

"But, you know the vitae of . . ."

"Divine grace works like good detergent. It cleans everything out!"

"I have a list of the saunas and bathrooms he used to visit and where he . . ."

"Forget it, my sweet."

"Prostitution is banned in my country and the law protects women. In Christian Europe . . ."

Accustomed to eavesdropping on cyber-chats, the subject of their conversation yawns. It's much the same nonsense in the Thereafter and the Hereafter! Wearing the orange peaked cap and missionary sandals that give him a harmless evangelical look, he rushes to his appointment arranged by High Command to plan the shantytown rebellion. To ward off possible spies who specialize in trailing putative Islamists, he is also carrying a beautifully bound edition of the Bible. He sits on a café terrace and placidly waits for his contact who will whisper the gang's password. The pigeons pecking around the Ludovicus Magnus Arch remind him of incidents and encounters from the old days. But he doesn't wallow in nostalgia and, savoring his Perrier *à la menthe*, he immerses himself in an uplifting reading of the first chapter of the Good Book, oblivious to the fact his acerbic rehearsal of the sketch with nude Eve and the thrusting Horny Rapper will put paid to his pathetic career as a terrorist.

THE ROOT OF ALL EVIL

Yes, I'm crazy about apples! I'll do anything to get my teeth into one! What can I say? That's me to a T, impulsive and irrational and whenever I see a tree laden with tasty fruit, I make a beeline that way and devour the fruit, oblivious to the consequences. My ex-partner whined: The Master forbids this, disobey him and you'll fuck up our eternal happiness! The idiot was unaware that this by-product of his own rib was to be the implacable scourge of humanity down the centuries. He followed the whimsical teachings from on high like a mule, convinced he'd live forever, never noticing that here below every Tom, Dick, and Harry dies and that's an end to their woes. But I knew the score the moment I put my head above the parapet and kept blasting him with my heresies.

Can't you see that what's corruptible in part is also corruptible in its entirety? What begins must end, and if you don't believe me, go ask your Maker, even though it's Sunday and he's having a little rest. What the hell did You do, ask Him, before You created this universe, this theme park where my lover-boy and I stroll around? Were You bored to tears, with Your head in the clouds? But the little fool from whom I was extracted was on his knees begging: no, no, He'll take revenge on us and we'll be hounded from paradise! What paradise are you on about, nitwit? The meadow where we graze like sheep? Bite that apple now or I'll stop screwing you and take off with the first skeptical beast to come my way! The would-be macho idiot whimpered like a lapdog, stunned by my tenacious, feminine caprice. He caved in, naturally he did! He shared the apple with yours truly and, aroused by its sour juices, with a little help on the side from the Viagra I bought at a drugstore and which I got him to swallow blind before tasting the fruit, we went through every coital trick illustrated in the *Kama Sutra*, exhaustively. They go on and on about my sentencing trillions of beings to death, but what the hell do I care?

THE CHERRY ON THE CAKE

The previous reflections of a "cherchez la femme" nature di-
vulged on the web page of a hostile splinter group stoke the anger of "Alice" and her colleagues in central command. The sketch
contradicts the religious, nationalist, and ideological orthodox-
ies of the groups they represent. The prophets, seers, and sages
who inspire them, and whose teachings they apply to the letter, have scant regard for the value of the female of the species,
although for reasons of political correctness they say quite the
opposite and preach respect for their dignity and reserve, hal-
lowed by tradition. The stubbornly deviationist positions on the
matter defended by our fall guy—possibly the fruit of an apos-
tasy and his desire for sabotage—undermine the foundations of

the organization and endanger its clandestine activities. Those gathered in conclave to analyze the case detect signs of collusion with the enemy and establish a list of crimes that may immediately lead him, with the full backing of the law, to the stake or the firing squad. But one cannot be too careful in these times of global, asymmetric war, in which the enemy refuses to acknowledge that the System is bankrupt and is struggling to survive with nothing more than the fury of those who know the writing is on the wall.

"Alice," the multiple agent, advises erring on the side of caution. The trap set to catch the offender must be honey-coated and cellophane-wrapped. Dressed like a society lady and appropriately made up, she rushes to look for him in order to establish contact with the exile from the Hereafter.

"Hello, 'Alice' here! Have I caught you at a bad moment? No? Well, let me tell you what this is about. I'm delighted with your hard work and discipline. We all are. Do you remember the mission we entrusted you with?"

"Setting the shantytowns on fire?"

"No, not yet. First you must go to the destination we will indicate for you in code. The objective is a conversation with the President. We're doing business with him, and our organization gives legal cover to his drug-carrying biplanes."

"But what if . . ."

"Forget your faggot scruples! His financial contribution to the cause is vital. Thirty percent of the gross value of all the heroin on the market! That's millions and millions, you know! It's an easy mission and our password will open all doors."

"Alice's" face disappears from the screen. The deceased has no desire whatsoever to travel to the other side of the Mediterranean as instructed by this geek, but is resigned to obeying. The hapless fellow doesn't know that "Alice"—unpredictable, devious "Alice"—immediately contacts the secret services of the country concerned to warn them of the imminent arrival of an intruder who loathes their philanthropic President and writes venomous pamphlets against his providential government!

FATHER OF THE FATHERLAND

I am the President's five senses! I observe everything that happens through his eyes, I use my subtle antennae to detect the slightest sign of discontent, I relish the precious powers he confers on me and stroke his likeness on the medal with which he decorated me. My service in his cause has no time restrictions: it even extends into my sleep. How often I have dreamed of a plot cooked up by his enemies and promptly intervened to nip it in the bud! Telephone bugging, secret maneuvers, surveillance cameras have woven the finest protective net, which allows me to give him any necessary information right on cue. My dispatches reach the palace daily and are a balsam to his restless heart. You should see his benign smile, his encouraging looks in my humble direction! Nothing that personal, obviously, but suggested by the official portraits that plaster the walls of my office that I linger to look at while organizing the demonstrations of support for his leadership or put together a list of malcontents. In the course of reading informers' reports and other confidential data, I look up and recharge my batteries on the sight of him saluting vertically with an arm wrapped in the flag of the fatherland. This inspires me and sends me into raptures! And I sometimes think I detect a personal smile directed especially at me. At other times, I intuit a knowing wink, betraying a discreet, austere tenderness. I collaborate in establishing his well-deserved good fortune and contribute with my ant-like scurrying to the consolidation of his providential government.

BRIBED

On orders from the High Command for Anti-System Resistance, he traveled to the destination as instructed, a state ruled with an iron hand by its almighty dictator. We aren't altogether sure if he arrived there by way of a charter company in the business of promoting the country's sun and heavenly beaches, or whether he covered the two thousand kilometers in one fell swoop, thanks to his weightless condition. What reliable sources have disclosed is that he was welcomed on the landing strip by a broad-shouldered, handlebar-mustachioed secret service officer who introduced himself forthwith as his guide and mentor. There's no rush for you to talk to our beloved President, he told him. While we organize an audience, I'll show you the places preferred by tourists and, if the opportunity arises, we'll fandango in a disco or two. The policeman seemed to want physical immediacy, gripped his arm affectionately, and, unexpectedly, commented on the beauty and passion of the local girls:

"I'll introduce you to one who says she knows you by sight. You know the one I mean?"

"Not a clue."

"The Horny Rapper! He's performing in our summer Festival with the top of the cream from Cannes and Locarno! Would you like to see her?"

"I, really . . ."

"Don't play hard to get! She's waiting for you just round the corner. I've rented a room for you in a luxury *meublé*. You'll be really comfortable there and, when you finish, I'll come and collect you."

Our hapless hero thinks he's living out a nightmare. The Rapper kisses him voraciously on the lips and forces him to test out the firmness of his breasts (that are not silicone, naturally, as he soon finds out) before dragging him off to a sordid hole with bidet, hand towels, and a bed that's been hurriedly remade and still stinks of semen and piss.

"If you're a real man, come with me! I'm on fire!"

The reader can imagine what happened next: there was no erection and, though spurred on, our deceased didn't come the cum. The Rapper insulted him in half a dozen languages and his screams brought the would-be guide and mentor to the scene. The broad-shouldered, handlebar-mustachioed policeman requisitioned two colleagues and the trio sodomized and abused him in turn as they filmed the inglorious scene on their cameras and cell phones.

That would teach the foulmouthed motherfucker to criticize the Chief's providential rule! That same night they would broadcast the video on TV if he didn't beg forgiveness for his unspeakable behavior and write an ode of praise in honor of the Leader of the Nation he had so insulted!

SELF-CRITICISM

When the Father of the People gave him an audience, the hapless scribbler confessed he was a complete fool. Only a fool like myself could (hoping to cause no offense, sir, I swear) have authored that unfortunate article that, as a result of its faulty rhetoric, solecisms, and amphibology, seemed to cast doubt upon the President's honest management of the public chest. I deserve to die a thousand deaths, I fully admit, but Your Excellency must forgive my lack of skill, my poverty-stricken training in grammar, the proverbial awkwardness and inanity of my writings. After off-loading his mea culpa, emboldened by the satrap's snores, he pulled his cap down, requisitioned a sword, looked askance, made his exit, and that was the end of that.

THE ONE AND ONLY

In the presidential elections periodically organized by my security services and in which I am backed in a plebiscite by 99.999% of the population, the scant number of votes against (less than a hundred from a census of more than ten million) persuaded me of the triumphant success of my governance ever since that now-distant day on which a providential armed movement hoisted me into the Leadership of the State and put an end to the charade of corrupt politicking rogues performing like puppets before an indignant, mocking public. Since then, everything has followed a perfect, orderly routine: the setting of a date for the referendum, a massive publicity campaign (city by city, district by district, household by household) for a yes-vote, a formal invitation for alternative candidacies to those who would like to compete against me and don't dare for fear of lasting opprobrium. The humiliating public excuses voiced by some of those pretentious poetasters dissuaded all the others from following their example and losing face in a laughable, pointless contest. But that isn't what happened in the last round of elections. There were no opponents, and the count, which was recorded and endorsed by a number of international observers, came up with an astonishing result: a single vote against.

After euphoric official celebrations, telegrams of congratulations from other Heads of State, and spontaneous street parties throughout the land, I confess I found the figure disturbing rather than comforting. It was quite normal for there to be a handful of resentful folk opposed to the great social achievements of my rule: they represented nothing more than their own blinkered and tragically uncomprehending viewpoints. But that solitary, hardline, obstinate vote, cast by someone so stubbornly opposed to my government's generosity, forewarned me of the existence of a new danger, of a latent threat that could surface at any moment.

Who was my enigmatic opponent?

I was obsessed by that question and couldn't sleep. I mobilized my information agencies to get on his trail and identify him: they must scrutinize the electoral district where the vote was cast, put the entire neighborhood under a microscope, establish a list of suspects, carefully sieve through the tapes filmed by the spy cameras on that ill-omened day. The search lasted several months and proved pointless. None of the individuals arrested on various round-ups admitted their guilt. Should there be recourse to torture of those jailed, as the head of the investigative team advised me? After weighing up the pros and cons, I concluded that this would be futile. Once submitted to such treatment, only the innocent would confess and, he, the relentless enemy of my good works, would give nothing away. Malevolently, implacably, he would redouble his efforts to fulfill his goal: to finish me off, that's right, to eliminate me.

I summoned my advisers and underlings in my command to discuss the matter. The ideas they put forward—individualized punishments from first to third degree, the extermination of all those on the electoral lists for the guilty district—seemed to me impracticable and I rejected every one of them. I had a dark feeling that this was a battle lost in advance. My merciless enemy would survive me. I suffered weeks of anguish, prey to a single idea: a secret, undetectable plot, in every intricate detail, was even now being put into place. As I tossed and turned in bed I had a dream full of foreboding: I saw myself in the polling center while I was casting the damned vote myself. When I woke up, without giving anyone prior notice, I filmed my confession on video, serenely certain that I would be executed immediately and then rest in peace forever.

FAGGOT, YOU FAGGOT

The benighted individual we are focusing on never wrote the ode of praise to the beloved President but he did pen, with a little help from us, the pages you have just read. Despite rigorous security measures around his figure and his isolation by the secret services, he vanished from his cell, probably via supernatural means that are beyond our comprehension. The fact is he's roaming the streets of his Le Sentier again, as cool as a freshly fished sardine—that barrio he likes to nose around where he always lived as an interloper and whence he passed on to a worse life, to the accompaniment of few tears and scant glory.

Unfortunately, the news of what happened in the brothel and a few compromising images are circulating on the Net and filling his spam can in the Hereafter. Given their outrageously macho and offensive character, we refuse to reproduce them in order to spare your blushes, dear reader. On the other hand, we *will* publicize an unexpected message of solidarity and support signed by Monsignor:

> Our Holy Mother the Apostolic, Roman Catholic Church warns us from the very beginning of the Bible against the temptations of the devil disguised as a woman. Some saints on the Christian calendar heroically resisted such seduction of the flesh and preferred self-emasculation to the indecent provocations of shameless hussies, like that Rapper or Flapper to whose charms my unjustly slighted friend did not yield. God recognizes his own. May he reward him with eternal glory.

Our quick-change artist smiles, and unfazed by his ambiguous state as the living dead or death warmed up, he settles in front of the computer that, dim as he is, he begins to operate skillfully, while waiting for a flash of incisive, if elusive, inspiration.

PROPOSAL FOR THE
MILLENNIUM FROM A DEAD WEB-SURFER

The genetic design laboratories that specialize in the comparative study of turtles have agreed, with the blessing of His Holiness and the great and the good in the System and Anti-System in the Thereafter, to initiate a bold project in line with the new European norms to reduce expenditure and abolish state spending and the taxes stifling the enterprises that generate wealth and work. The scientific analysis of the behavior of turtles and their annual periods of hibernation would allow the creation of a mechanism that could be readily adapted to the citizenry by dint of which the non-productive, needy classes could opt in a pilot program of unquestionable value to enter a state of wintry lethargy that would spare them the need to hunt for a crust of bread during the harshest months of the year, with subsequent savings in capital and human suffering. The creation of comfortable dormitory sheds for those helped in this way would considerably reduce the budget imbalance that's slowing down the economy's recovery as well as encourage the competitiveness of our consortia in the savage scramble for loot in the Global Village.

THE SANHEDRIN

He received an e-mail with the acronym of one of "Alice's" countless pseudonyms: a summons to an urgent meeting of the Pro-
Peace and Tolerance management committee that was going to
discuss "the necessary procedures for the establishing of a flow-
chart for future actions." The content and lexis of the message left
him nonplussed. Did it relate to the previous qualitative leap in
their general offensive against the System? Or was it simply a ploy
to attract the attention of Interpol and send it on a wild-goose
chase? He was totally in the dark. Despite his growing feeling of
mistrust, reeling after so many blows and beatings at the hands
of the redeeming cause in which he'd enlisted, he bit the bullet
and headed to the dark, discreet back alley frequented in his past
gallivanting by junkies and prostitutes. He struggled up the spiral

staircase to the attic (the years don't pass in vain, even in the Hereafter!), and as he pushed open the door to his appointment, plastered with stickers in Quechua, Kurdish, and Basque, he was surprised by the theatrical layout, the carefully arranged scenario: a platform with half a dozen speakers looking severely judgmental (he would soon discover that judges they were!) or dressed as *guerrilleros*, and, at its foot, a bandy-legged plastic chair where he was ordered to sit down.

The indictment drawn up in secret contained extremely serious accusations. "Alice" was sporting his turban and hennaed beard, the rabbi in his hat and Rasta dreadlocks was forcefully straightening his spectacles, and Monsignor adopted the seraphic stance of the saints he worshipped. Next to them stood three militants from the Anti-System Commandos or other groups it was impossible to identify, hidden as they were in their hoods like the hostage-decapitators on TV!

"Alice," our mutant, devious "Alice" took on the prosecutor's role unabashed:

"What has happened in the course of the operation entrusted to our ex-comrade present here contravenes the ethical code and elementary principles of the Organization, endangering both it and the safety of its members and objectively suiting the strategy of . . ."

Et cetera, et cetera, et cetera.

But the charge slides easily off the skin of the accused. His experience of Hereafter and Thereafter, or Thereafter and Hereafter, has covered him in scales, given him the shell of a little tortoise. He repeatedly whispers the name of Spinoza (a surprise with a capital S: our character had hidden his philosophical leanings up to this point!), as if the succession of setbacks has put an end to his resignation and strengthened his spirit. He can hear the accusations and evidence being trotted out, but isn't listening. Though he did heed the Monsignor's intervention . . . Bored, he was expecting a defense in line with his encouraging e-mail, but how wrong he was. The Beloved of Jesus Christ via Little Boys, flirtatiously wrapped in his prelate's cape, impassively invoked the divine punishment of the accursed cities, the church's condemnation of the abominable sin. A *guerrillero* with a Caribbean lilt spoke of libidinous and political deviationism . . . The hooded leader of the Direct Action Commandos spoke of the wiles the System employed to detect the contradictions and weak points of our petty-bourgeois comrades . . . But he understood not a jot of what the self-styled Commissar of the Red Dragons came out with: he spoke in Japanese, if not Chinese!

When he emerged from his nirvana, "Alice" was reading out his sentence. In view of the gravity of the charges against him, the court was unanimously sentencing him to the maximum penalty, although it would leave its execution in his own hands. After handing over the pistol he should use to end his days, one by one the judges abandoned the attic without so much as a good-bye.

"Alice" and her sidekicks haven't the slightest idea that they have ceased to be our characters, and that we won't see them ever again! Our protagonist stares at his weapon and turns it all over time and again in his brain. Dear reader, it is no laughing matter. Let's inject a bit of logic: how the hell does a dead man commit suicide?

FINAL E-MAIL

Feeling abandoned? Don't yield to melancholy and despair. Let us manage your soul. We don't suggest martyrdom to redeem you from your sins nor tell you what sort of arsenal is necessary to carry it out: a belt of explosives, machine gun, CETME rifle, or Kalashnikov. Indeed, we won't even give you a manual giving instructions for the manufacture of chemical substances destined to sow terror among apostates, heretics, and opportunists.

We have a much cleaner weapon: Love. If you listen to us and choose the righteous path, you will emerge at a single stroke from so much infamy and dross. The light of transcendence will shine down on you. You will rise weightlessly above this world of shady business and hateful doctrines. The siren songs of the extremists won't affect you. Exalted by Grace, you will levitate like one of these starry molecules that enjoy a first-hand vision of their Maker. The embarrassing episodes in your life will be erased all at once and you will be reborn blameless and stainless. The benefits will be infinite. We will show you the way. Just give us your credit card and bank account numbers, and we will work diligently at turning your dream into reality.

(Anonymous)

THAT'S SHIT NO PANTS CAN HANDLE

Who'd gone more insane, the world or him? Our scribbler isn't sure he can come up with the answer, and neither are we. Everything he'd fantasized about as time went by now appears before his eyes as a metaphor for an inexorably sick reality. The level of the seas is rising, ethnic shantytowns are burning, and terrorism is spreading and is trivialized in the name of divine, inflammatory curses and grotesque emotions all prompted by identity crises. Everything is bought and sold as in clearance sales organized by gambling addicts. Mafiosi, councillors, and real-estate promoters (of loathsome Golf Resorts) are forging a quite unholy alliance around bricks and mortar. The coarsest morsel of private life invades the public sphere and the brutalized inhabitants of our insignificant marble only seem to exist as news items.

The melancholy of our marooned guy with the sad countenance changes nonetheless to exasperation when he glimpses the flag of the Chechen-slaughtering Czar in the depths of the Arctic, as a prelude to his merciless exploitation of the energy resources there. The vast shelf of ice was the refuge of his dreams and he had mentally located his solitary hearth there, far from any annoying interference! Given his innate tendency to tell tales, he composes scenes and farces to make up for his exhaustion and despondency. But none of that can console him for the worrying lack of transcendence in his two-way journey between death and life.

While the author writes these lines, they both gaze at the beautiful bay of the city where they've met by chance, and the panorama of its two shores: the ferries coming and going with their burden of nostalgia and dreams; the summer holidays of latter-day Ulysseses sporting caps, Bermuda shorts, and fake designer T-shirts at the steering wheels of delivery vans and cars with roof racks piled high with furniture, bicycles, and all manner of chattel. Things seemed to be functioning like a well-oiled set of comic sketches in a great theater of flags blowing in the wind. But you only had to look away toward the wastelands and empty lots near the port to catch sight of gangs of kids sniffing glue-soaked handkerchiefs. Our scribbler would have liked to live like them, amid the trash and rats, in the pristine glory of a truncated childhood. Although we were afraid he might join a gang and disappear into one of its hideouts, this wasn't the case. He vanished in a flash and, led by a hunch that proved to be correct, we came across him, more than half a century ago, in the city of his future, and by now of his past, loitering, a busybody and Peeping Tom.

HE ADDS HIS PERSONAL TOUCH
TO THE FRENZIED CHAOS OF THE UNIVERSE

From his shattered projection into the Hereafter, the protagonist of these pages spends the occasional moment evoking in the virtual world incidents and loves from his barren life in the Thereafter hitherto silenced by his modesty and inhibitions: for example, his liking for the piano and his secret ambition to compose sonatas worthy of the great Amadeus.

When he abandoned his country of origin (the name of which we cannot pass on to the reader, because he never mentions it) and traveled to the city of his dreams (that city where he vegetated uselessly for more than forty years), he ended up marooned in a boardinghouse run by a former singer whose lodgers shared her devotion to the most noble and ethereal of the Arts. Our Little Monster (he'd just hit twenty!) gave himself up to melancholy bouts of listening to the works of Satie, performed by his fellow lodgers (the *Gymnopédies*, *Trois morceaux en forme de poire*, *Trois valses distinguées du précieux dégoûté*) and took advantage of merciful moments provided by the absence of witnesses (when his roommates were out and the penniless diva went to say her prayers in the nearby church) to sit at the piano and play the scores on the keyboard with nervous fingers, though his knowledge of scales was extremely rocky. He convinced himself he was Satie, overcome by a clearly grotesque rush of emotion to his head. He foresaw that he too would scorn traditional forms and that the trash he'd pen would adopt the rough shape of an acorn or dried fig. He identified with Debussy's unruly friend, with his contempt for social life and artistic conventions. He was born clumsy and would remain so till the bitter end. Ah! You just see, when you hit sixty! Satie's friends warned, and, like him, he'd long ago passed the so-called age of reason and sound knowledge, and had seen nothing at all apart from his pitiful contribution to the disarray and madness in the universe.

ALONE ONCE MORE

The man unjustly dubbed the Monster (and we'll stop calling him that from now on) has returned to his old hunting ground. His skirmish with the System and Anti-System has ended in total failure. He now expects nothing from this world or the next. He knows them both and prefers a limbo where he can stay forever in a quietly distracting gloaming. But ineffable Benedict the Antiquated, he of the throne and Popemobile, has just deprogrammed the place, so he has no choice but to roam the back alleys of his barrio. He no longer waits with his little white mouse for little girls as they leave school, like his would-be alter ego in the Thereafter. Nor does he spy on brawny types brazenly rubbing their crotches and twirling their mustaches in public bathrooms. All *that* belongs to a real or imaginary past alien to his present state. Perhaps he's a hard liver or a diehard, like his author, but he feels he is free. He's not searching for anything and has no need to adopt the disguise of gabardine, hat, and tinted glasses. He is transparent, and when his tiresome ex-neighbor bumps into him in their boulevard, she can't see him or launch into her usual spiel about the fifth column of Moorish-African immigrants. He can also see from afar the media philosopher whose portrait he penned on page 11, and the gleeful paladin of Forza Italia, intoxicated by the latest triumphs of *Il Cavaliere*. He has no need to put possible enemies off his trail: everybody ignores him. He walks across the place for contracting casual labor, and gives them a wide berth. His shoes lead him to the street that lends its name to the neighborhood and stops in front of the fine building at number eight, which is now a store for wholesale clothes merchants. He looks up and his eyes linger on a modest commemorative plaque. Mozart lived there, with Maria, his mother, in 1781. The thought moves him. If he were flesh and blood, tears would cloud his eyes. But he isn't, and he continues his usual prying, shoe-leather punishing route while he gazes at himself in the Hereafter, on his computer screen.

BORN BEFORE MY TIME

I desperately wanted to be Mozart, but it was not to be. I was born in 1756 BC and there were no musical instruments or lessons in those inhospitable days. Nevertheless, a clear intuition of his art dwelled in me, as I told members of the clan I belonged to, and they then insulted me and called me a liar. At the age of eight I drew a piano in the sand on the heath and it was mercilessly erased by the wind despite all my precautions. I composed my first sonatas in my poor brain, though I couldn't perform them for lack of the proper equipment. I dreamed of a place like Salzburg or the Court in Vienna but could only see adobe huts and the pools where my fellow countrymen slaked their thirst alongside their animals on the vast plain before me. The day I tried to conduct the overture to *The Magic Flute*, my gesticulations provoked the ire of the tribal elders and our head shaman. I was tried by a court of wise men and sentenced to death. While they grabbed me and tied me to a stake stuck in the ground, I had time to sing the first bars of an aria from *Don Giovanni* with my imaginary contralto voice. The heat from the flames prevented me from continuing.

FROM NOTHING TO NOTHING

The disconcerted novelist who wrote the book leafs through the pages of the newspapers looking for his obituary. What will it say about him? He does so secretly hoping he will spot errors, notice anachronisms and questionable dates; that the piece has attributed to him the outstanding features of someone else's life: works written by others or never written at all; confused or invented roots, studies, travels, and family. That he had been someone else, a fictional entity whose labors and excursions might relieve and surprise him. The truth of his story is held in the words. All that would remain of him would be the dream of a derisory existence. Of a tailless shooting star, sentenced by the world's sound and fury to sudden, silent extinction.

GOOD-BYE

Dear reader, the time has come to say good-bye. Everything runs its course, including time itself, and from the glimmer of a remote, undetectable galaxy, we behold you and the hapless hero of these pages with benign pity. His life in the Hereafter has been as useless as the one compiled in the massive tome on his stomping around Le Sentier. Attempts to enquire about the reasons for his entry into the world and his abrupt exit thence shattered against the fiction and absurdity of everything around us. An infinite set of reflections about our transit through somewhere that's condemned to be nowhere can hardly elucidate the enigma of such a parasitic existence. His irremediably thickheaded stubbornness and nil practicality have, as you know, endeared him to us.

An "I want my money back, I've understood nothing" of a kindred spirit, who expresses his confusion at the end of the performance. But no need to have any regrets, nobody is guilty of any crime. Pettiness is our saving grace: that exquisite mix of meaninglessness and resolve.

For Abdul-Haq, who came unsolicited
into the world and left it equally unaware.

Born in 1931, JUAN GOYTISOLO went into voluntary exile in 1956 and has never returned to live in Spain. A bitter opponent of the Franco regime, his early novels were banned in his native country. He divided his time between Paris and Marrakesh until the death of his wife, Monique Lange, at which time he moved permanently to Marrakesh.

PETER BUSH has translated ten books by Juan Goytisolo, including *Juan the Landless*, as well as novels by other prominent Spanish and Latin American writers such as Juan Carlos Onetti and Ramón del Valle-Inclán.

SELECTED DALKEY ARCHIVE PAPERBACKS

PETROS ABATZOGLOU, *What Does Mrs.*
Freeman Want?
MICHAL AJVAZ, *The Golden Age.*
The Other City.
PIERRE ALBERT-BIROT, *Grabinoulor.*
YUZ ALESHKOVSKY, *Kangaroo.*
FELIPE ALFAU, *Chromos.*
Locos.
IVAN ÂNGELO, *The Celebration.*
The Tower of Glass.
DAVID ANTIN, *Talking.*
ANTÓNIO LOBO ANTUNES,
Knowledge of Hell.
ALAIN ARIAS-MISSON, *Theatre of Incest.*
IFTIKHAR ARIF AND WAQAS KHWAJA, EDS.,
Modern Poetry of Pakistan.
JOHN ASHBERY AND JAMES SCHUYLER,
A Nest of Ninnies.
GABRIELA AVIGUR-ROTEM, *Heatwave*
and Crazy Birds.
HEIMRAD BÄCKER, *transcript.*
DJUNA BARNES, *Ladies Almanack.*
Ryder.
JOHN BARTH, *LETTERS.*
Sabbatical.
DONALD BARTHELME, *The King.*
Paradise.
SVETISLAV BASARA, *Chinese Letter.*
RENÉ BELLETTO, *Dying.*
MARK BINELLI, *Sacco and Vanzetti*
Must Die!
ANDREI BITOV, *Pushkin House.*
ANDREJ BLATNIK, *You Do Understand.*
LOUIS PAUL BOON, *Chapel Road.*
My Little War.
Summer in Termuren
ROGER BOYLAN, *Killoyle.*
IGNÁCIO DE LOYOLA BRANDÃO,
Anonymous Celebrity.
The Good-Bye Angel.
Teeth under the Sun.
Zero.
BONNIE BREMSER,
Troia: Mexican Memoirs.
CHRISTINE BROOKE-ROSE, *Amalgamemnon.*
BRIGID BROPHY, *In Transit.*
MEREDITH BROSNAN, *Mr. Dynamite.*
GERALD L. BRUNS, *Modern Poetry and*
the Idea of Language.
EVGENY BUNIMOVICH AND J. KATES, EDS.,
Contemporary Russian Poetry.
An Anthology.
GABRIELLE BURTON, *Heartbreak Hotel.*
MICHEL BUTOR, *Degrees.*
Mobile.
Portrait of the Artist as a Young Ape.
G. CABRERA INFANTE, *Infante's Inferno.*
Three Trapped Tigers.
JULIETA CAMPOS,
The Fear of Losing Eurydice.
ANNE CARSON, *Eros the Bittersweet.*
ORLY CASTEL-BLOOM, *Dolly City.*
CAMILO JOSÉ CELA, *Christ versus Arizona.*
The Family of Pascual Duarte.
The Hive.
LOUIS-FERDINAND CÉLINE, *Castle to Castle.*
Conversations with Professor Y.
London Bridge.
Normance.

North.
Rigadoon.
HUGO CHARTERIS, *The Tide Is Right.*
JEROME CHARYN, *The Tar Baby.*
ERIC CHEVILLARD, *Demolishing Nisard.*
MARC CHOLODENKO, *Mordechai Schamz.*
JOSHUA COHEN, *Witz.*
EMILY HOLMES COLEMAN, *The Shutter*
of Snow.
ROBERT COOVER, *A Night at the Movies.*
STANLEY CRAWFORD, *Log of the S.S. The*
Mrs Unguentine.
Some Instructions to My Wife.
ROBERT CREELEY, *Collected Prose.*
RENÉ CREVEL, *Putting My Foot in It.*
RALPH CUSACK, *Cadenza.*
SUSAN DAITCH, *L.C.*
Storytown.
NICHOLAS DELBANCO,
The Count of Concord.
Sherbrookes.
NIGEL DENNIS, *Cards of Identity.*
PETER DIMOCK, *A Short Rhetoric for*
Leaving the Family.
ARIEL DORFMAN, *Konfidenz.*
COLEMAN DOWELL,
The Houses of Children.
Island People.
Too Much Flesh and Jabez.
ARKADII DRAGOMOSHCHENKO, *Dust.*
RIKKI DUCORNET, *The Complete*
Butcher's Tales.
The Fountains of Neptune.
The Jade Cabinet.
The One Marvelous Thing.
Phosphor in Dreamland
The Stain.
The Word "Desire."
WILLIAM EASTLAKE, *The Bamboo Bed.*
Castle Keep.
Lyric of the Circle Heart.
JEAN ECHENOZ, *Chopin's Move.*
STANLEY ELKIN, *A Bad Man.*
Boswell: A Modern Comedy.
Criers and Kibitzers, Kibitzers
and Criers.
The Dick Gibson Show.
The Franchiser.
George Mills.
The Living End.
The MacGuffin.
The Magic Kingdom.
Mrs. Ted Bliss.
The Rabbi of Lud.
Van Gogh's Room at Arles.
ANNIE ERNAUX, *Cleaned Out.*
LAUREN FAIRBANKS, *Muzzle Thyself.*
Sister Carrie.
LESLIE A. FIEDLER, *Love and Death in*
the American Novel.
JUAN FILLOY, *Op Oloop.*
GUSTAVE FLAUBERT, *Bouvard and Pécuchet.*
KASS FLEISHER, *Talking out of School.*
FORD MADOX FORD,
The March of Literature.
JON FOSSE, *Aliss at the Fire.*
Melancholy.
MAX FRISCH, *I'm Not Stiller.*
Man in the Holocene.

FOR A FULL LIST OF PUBLICATIONS, VISIT:
www.dalkeyarchive.com

SELECTED DALKEY ARCHIVE PAPERBACKS

CARLOS FUENTES, *Christopher Unborn.*
  Distant Relations.
  Terra Nostra.
  Where the Air Is Clear.
JANICE GALLOWAY, *Foreign Parts.*
  The Trick Is to Keep Breathing.
WILLIAM H. GASS, *Cartesian Sonata*
  and Other Novellas.
  Finding a Form.
  A Temple of Texts.
  The Tunnel.
  Willie Masters' Lonesome Wife.
GÉRARD GAVARRY, *Hoppla! 1 2 3.*
  Making a Novel.
ETIENNE GILSON,
  The Arts of the Beautiful.
  Forms and Substances in the Arts.
C. S. GISCOMBE, *Giscome Road.*
  Here.
  Prairie Style.
DOUGLAS GLOVER, *Bad News of the Heart.*
  The Enamoured Knight.
WITOLD GOMBROWICZ,
  A Kind of Testament.
KAREN ELIZABETH GORDON,
  The Red Shoes.
GEORGI GOSPODINOV, *Natural Novel.*
JUAN GOYTISOLO, *Count Julian.*
  Exiled from Almost Everywhere.
  Juan the Landless.
  Makbara.
  Marks of Identity.
PATRICK GRAINVILLE, *The Cave of Heaven.*
HENRY GREEN, *Back.*
  Blindness.
  Concluding.
  Doting.
  Nothing.
JIŘÍ GRUŠA, *The Questionnaire.*
GABRIEL GUDDING,
  Rhode Island Notebook.
MELA HARTWIG, *Am I a Redundant*
  Human Being?
JOHN HAWKES, *The Passion Artist.*
  Whistlejacket.
ALEKSANDAR HEMON, ED.,
  Best European Fiction.
AIDAN HIGGINS, *A Bestiary.*
  Balcony of Europe.
  Bornholm Night-Ferry.
  Darkling Plain: Texts for the Air.
  Flotsam and Jetsam.
  Langrishe, Go Down.
  Scenes from a Receding Past.
  Windy Arbours.
KEIZO HINO, *Isle of Dreams.*
KAZUSHI HOSAKA, *Plainsong.*
ALDOUS HUXLEY, *Antic Hay.*
  Crome Yellow.
  Point Counter Point.
  Those Barren Leaves.
  Time Must Have a Stop.
NAOYUKI II, *The Shadow of a Blue Cat.*
MIKHAIL IOSSEL AND JEFF PARKER, EDS.,
  Amerika: Russian Writers View the
  United States.
GERT JONKE, *The Distant Sound.*
  Geometric Regional Novel.
  Homage to Czerny.
  The System of Vienna.

JACQUES JOUET, *Mountain R.*
  Savage.
  Upstaged.
CHARLES JULIET, *Conversations with*
  Samuel Beckett and Bram van
  Velde.
MIEKO KANAI, *The Word Book.*
YORAM KANIUK, *Life on Sandpaper.*
HUGH KENNER, *The Counterfeiters.*
  Flaubert, Joyce and Beckett:
  The Stoic Comedians.
  Joyce's Voices.
DANILO KIŠ, *Garden, Ashes.*
  A Tomb for Boris Davidovich.
ANITA KONKKA, *A Fool's Paradise.*
GEORGE KONRÁD, *The City Builder.*
TADEUSZ KONWICKI, *A Minor Apocalypse.*
  The Polish Complex.
MENIS KOUMANDAREAS, *Koula.*
ELAINE KRAF, *The Princess of 72nd Street.*
JIM KRUSOE, *Iceland.*
EWA KURYLUK, *Century 21.*
EMILIO LASCANO TEGUI, *On Elegance*
  While Sleeping.
ERIC LAURRENT, *Do Not Touch.*
HERVÉ LE TELLIER, *The Sextine Chapel.*
  A Thousand Pearls (for a Thousand
  Pennies)
VIOLETTE LEDUC, *La Bâtarde.*
EDOUARD LEVÉ, *Suicide.*
SUZANNE JILL LEVINE, *The Subversive*
  Scribe: Translating Latin
  American Fiction.
DEBORAH LEVY, *Billy and Girl.*
  Pillow Talk in Europe and Other
  Places.
JOSÉ LEZAMA LIMA, *Paradiso.*
ROSA LIKSOM, *Dark Paradise.*
OSMAN LINS, *Avalovara.*
  The Queen of the Prisons of Greece.
ALF MAC LOCHLAINN,
  The Corpus in the Library.
  Out of Focus.
RON LOEWINSOHN, *Magnetic Field(s).*
MINA LOY, *Stories and Essays of Mina Loy.*
BRIAN LYNCH, *The Winner of Sorrow.*
D. KEITH MANO, *Take Five.*
MICHELINE AHARONIAN MARCOM,
  The Mirror in the Well.
BEN MARCUS,
  The Age of Wire and String.
WALLACE MARKFIELD,
  Teitlebaum's Window.
  To an Early Grave.
DAVID MARKSON, *Reader's Block.*
  Springer's Progress.
  Wittgenstein's Mistress.
CAROLE MASO, *AVA.*
LADISLAV MATEJKA AND KRYSTYNA
  POMORSKA, EDS.,
  Readings in Russian Poetics:
  Formalist and Structuralist Views.
HARRY MATHEWS,
  The Case of the Persevering Maltese:
  Collected Essays.
  Cigarettes.
  The Conversions.
  The Human Country: New and
  Collected Stories.
  The Journalist.

FOR A FULL LIST OF PUBLICATIONS, VISIT:
www.dalkeyarchive.com

SELECTED DALKEY ARCHIVE PAPERBACKS

My Life in CIA.
Singular Pleasures.
The Sinking of the Odradek
Stadium.
Tlooth.
20 Lines a Day.
JOSEPH MCELROY,
Night Soul and Other Stories.
THOMAS MCGONIGLE,
Going to Patchogue.
ROBERT L. MCLAUGHLIN, ED., *Innovations:*
An Anthology of
Modern & Contemporary Fiction.
ABDELWAHAB MEDDEB, *Talismano.*
HERMAN MELVILLE, *The Confidence-Man.*
AMANDA MICHALOPOULOU, *I'd Like.*
STEVEN MILLHAUSER,
The Barnum Museum.
In the Penny Arcade.
RALPH J. MILLS, JR.,
Essays on Poetry.
MOMUS, *The Book of Jokes.*
CHRISTINE MONTALBETTI, *Western.*
OLIVE MOORE, *Spleen.*
NICHOLAS MOSLEY, *Accident.*
Assassins.
Catastrophe Practice.
Children of Darkness and Light.
Experience and Religion.
God's Hazard.
The Hesperides Tree.
Hopeful Monsters.
Imago Bird.
Impossible Object.
Inventing God.
Judith.
Look at the Dark.
Natalie Natalia.
Paradoxes of Peace.
Serpent.
Time at War.
The Uses of Slime Mould:
Essays of Four Decades.
WARREN MOTTE,
Fables of the Novel: French Fiction
since 1990.
Fiction Now: The French Novel in
the 21st Century.
Oulipo: A Primer of Potential
Literature.
YVES NAVARRE, *Our Share of Time.*
Sweet Tooth.
DOROTHY NELSON, *In Night's City.*
Tar and Feathers.
ESHKOL NEVO, *Homesick.*
WILFRIDO D. NOLLEDO, *But for the Lovers.*
FLANN O'BRIEN,
At Swim-Two-Birds.
At War.
The Best of Myles.
The Dalkey Archive.
Further Cuttings.
The Hard Life.
The Poor Mouth.
The Third Policeman.
CLAUDE OLLIER, *The Mise-en-Scène.*
Wert and the Life Without End.
PATRIK OUŘEDNÍK, *Europeana.*
The Opportune Moment, 1855.
BORIS PAHOR, *Necropolis.*

FERNANDO DEL PASO,
News from the Empire.
Palinuro of Mexico.
ROBERT PINGET, *The Inquisitory.*
Mahu or The Material.
Trio.
MANUEL PUIG,
Betrayed by Rita Hayworth.
The Buenos Aires Affair.
Heartbreak Tango.
RAYMOND QUENEAU, *The Last Days.*
Odile.
Pierrot Mon Ami.
Saint Glinglin.
ANN QUIN, *Berg.*
Passages.
Three.
Tripticks.
ISHMAEL REED,
The Free-Lance Pallbearers.
The Last Days of Louisiana Red.
Ishmael Reed: The Plays.
Juice!
Reckless Eyeballing.
The Terrible Threes.
The Terrible Twos.
Yellow Back Radio Broke-Down.
JOÃO UBALDO RIBEIRO, *House of the*
Fortunate Buddhas.
JEAN RICARDOU, *Place Names.*
RAINER MARIA RILKE, *The Notebooks of*
Malte Laurids Brigge.
JULIÁN RÍOS, *The House of Ulysses.*
Larva: A Midsummer Night's Babel.
Poundemonium.
Procession of Shadows.
AUGUSTO ROA BASTOS, *I the Supreme.*
DANIËL ROBBERECHTS,
Arriving in Avignon.
JEAN ROLIN, *The Explosion of the*
Radiator Hose.
OLIVIER ROLIN, *Hotel Crystal.*
ALIX CLEO ROUBAUD, *Alix's Journal.*
JACQUES ROUBAUD, *The Form of a*
City Changes Faster, Alas, Than
the Human Heart.
The Great Fire of London.
Hortense in Exile.
Hortense Is Abducted.
The Loop.
The Plurality of Worlds of Lewis.
The Princess Hoppy.
Some Thing Black.
LEON S. ROUDIEZ, *French Fiction Revisited.*
RAYMOND ROUSSEL, *Impressions of Africa.*
VEDRANA RUDAN, *Night.*
STIG SÆTERBAKKEN, *Siamese.*
LYDIE SALVAYRE, *The Company of Ghosts.*
Everyday Life.
The Lecture.
Portrait of the Writer as a
Domesticated Animal.
The Power of Flies.
LUIS RAFAEL SÁNCHEZ,
Macho Camacho's Beat.
SEVERO SARDUY, *Cobra & Maitreya.*
NATHALIE SARRAUTE,
Do You Hear Them?
Martereau.
The Planetarium.

FOR A FULL LIST OF PUBLICATIONS, VISIT:
www.dalkeyarchive.com

ARNO SCHMIDT, *Collected Novellas.*
Collected Stories.
Nobodaddy's Children.
Two Novels.
ASAF SCHURR, *Motti.*
CHRISTINE SCHUTT, *Nightwork.*
GAIL SCOTT, *My Paris.*
DAMION SEARLS, *What We Were Doing and Where We Were Going.*
JUNE AKERS SEESE, *Is This What Other Women Feel Too?*
What Waiting Really Means.
BERNARD SHARE, *Inish.*
Transit.
AURELIE SHEEHAN, *Jack Kerouac Is Pregnant.*
VIKTOR SHKLOVSKY, *Bowstring.*
Knight's Move.
A Sentimental Journey: Memoirs 1917–1922.
Energy of Delusion: A Book on Plot.
Literature and Cinematography.
Theory of Prose.
Third Factory.
Zoo, or Letters Not about Love.
CLAUDE SIMON, *The Invitation.*
PIERRE SINIAC, *The Collaborators.*
JOSEF ŠKVORECKÝ, *The Engineer of Human Souls.*
GILBERT SORRENTINO, *Aberration of Starlight.*
Blue Pastoral.
Crystal Vision.
Imaginative Qualities of Actual Things.
Mulligan Stew.
Pack of Lies.
Red the Fiend.
The Sky Changes.
Something Said.
Splendide-Hôtel.
Steelwork.
Under the Shadow.
W. M. SPACKMAN, *The Complete Fiction.*
ANDRZEJ STASIUK, *Fado.*
GERTRUDE STEIN, *Lucy Church Amiably.*
The Making of Americans.
A Novel of Thank You.
LARS SVENDSEN, *A Philosophy of Evil.*
PIOTR SZEWC, *Annihilation.*
GONÇALO M. TAVARES, *Jerusalem.*
Learning to Pray in the Age of Technology.
LUCIAN DAN TEODOROVICI, *Our Circus Presents . . .*
STEFAN THEMERSON, *Hobson's Island.*
The Mystery of the Sardine.
Tom Harris.
JOHN TOOMEY, *Sleepwalker.*
JEAN-PHILIPPE TOUSSAINT, *The Bathroom.*
Camera.
Monsieur.
Running Away.
Self-Portrait Abroad.
Television.
DUMITRU TSEPENEAG, *Hotel Europa.*

The Necessary Marriage.
Pigeon Post.
Vain Art of the Fugue.
ESTHER TUSQUETS, *Stranded.*
DUBRAVKA UGRESIC, *Lend Me Your Character.*
Thank You for Not Reading.
MATI UNT, *Brecht at Night.*
Diary of a Blood Donor.
Things in the Night.
ÁLVARO URIBE AND OLIVIA SEARS, EDS., *Best of Contemporary Mexican Fiction.*
ELOY URROZ, *Friction.*
The Obstacles.
LUISA VALENZUELA, *Dark Desires and the Others.*
He Who Searches.
MARJA-LIISA VARTIO, *The Parson's Widow.*
PAUL VERHAEGHEN, *Omega Minor.*
BORIS VIAN, *Heartsnatcher.*
LLORENÇ VILLALONGA, *The Dolls' Room.*
ORNELA VORPSI, *The Country Where No One Ever Dies.*
AUSTRYN WAINHOUSE, *Hedyphagetica.*
PAUL WEST, *Words for a Deaf Daughter & Gala.*
CURTIS WHITE, *America's Magic Mountain.*
The Idea of Home.
Memories of My Father Watching TV.
Monstrous Possibility: An Invitation to Literary Politics.
Requiem.
DIANE WILLIAMS, *Excitability: Selected Stories.*
Romancer Erector.
DOUGLAS WOOLF, *Wall to Wall.*
Ya! & John-Juan.
JAY WRIGHT, *Polynomials and Pollen.*
The Presentable Art of Reading Absence.
PHILIP WYLIE, *Generation of Vipers.*
MARGUERITE YOUNG, *Angel in the Forest.*
Miss MacIntosh, My Darling.
REYOUNG, *Unbabbling.*
VLADO ŽABOT, *The Succubus.*
ZORAN ŽIVKOVIĆ, *Hidden Camera.*
LOUIS ZUKOFSKY, *Collected Fiction.*
SCOTT ZWIREN, *God Head.*